THE
CLEANSING

STEVEN GREEN

authorHOUSE®

AuthorHouse™
1663 Liberty Drive
Bloomington, IN 47403
www.authorhouse.com
Phone: 1 (800) 839-8640

Published by AuthorHouse 09/16/2019

ISBN: 978-1-7283-2636-8 (sc)
ISBN: 978-1-7283-2635-1 (e)

Print information available on the last page.

This book is printed on acid-free paper.

Dedicated to:

My friends and family who
I subjected to multiple readings.
B.S.A 653

CHAPTER 1

"ARE WE THERE YET?" It was a question asked a hundred times in the past week. It had become part of a never ending game between the kids and the adults.

"About another hour" was the reply.

Tom whispered to john" aren't you tired of this game yet?" John new that this time it was different, this time, it was true.

"Dave, follow the creek another quarter mile and you will come to a feeder stream. Take that stream and follow it until you come to a clearing. We'll camp there. Everybody, stay in the stream the rest of the way. I'll bring up the rear."

Everyone stepped into the stream from the same large rock as they had done all week.

John stayed back until the last person got in. Then, he started erasing the tracks as he had done so many times before. Only this time, it was different. This time it meant the difference between life and death. If anyone was following their trail, he needed them to get lost here. He walked back down the trail a little way and started. First, he made it look like they entered the stream and exited the other side. Then he slowly and meticulously erased the trail that they did take. John knew that a real tracker would still be able to follow them but he was counting on the fact that most of them were common folks and not experienced hunters.

Who would have figured that six weeks ago everyone here was just an average American who busied their lives with day to day living. Then, the unthinkable. A terrorist plot two years in the making. It was simple by design, cruel by intention and it grew like a wildfire in a tinder dry climate. The plan, eliminate the white man from the earth. The timing, Sept. 11, the anniversary of the trade center attack. The soldiers, all the oppressed people in America who blamed the white man for their troubles. Al Queida had sent messengers to all the leaders. They enlisted help from the Indians, blacks, Mexicans, middle easterners, and anyone else they thought might be sympathetic to their cause. The timing was perfect. America was in the midst of an economic recession that had lasted for almost six years. First, they blamed the Republicans for the problems. Then, they blamed all white man for the problems and like a farmer, they planted the seed of rebellion and waited. They waited until the time was right to harvest.

When the American government found out that the threat was "verifiable and real", they decided to keep it quiet and not let the general public know. "no sense in causing a panic. The military can defend the public if this does happen" What they didn't count on was the vast numbers of oppressed people in the service siding against America.

The rumor had been around for a couple of years but was always dismissed as just that, a rumor. Only when the government finally verified the threat did they alert the necessary people on a need to know basis. The media was kept in the dark along with the general population. The only people who knew were the military, national guard, and the state police. The local police were simply told that something "might" happen in the near future.

Mark was a lieutenant in the state police in charge of the gang unit. He was briefed to the "possibility of certain events" by the governor and sworn to secrecy. Mark had a hard time comprehending the severity of the situation at first but once it sunk in, he knew he had to act. He decided to gather a group of families to escape the madness. He chose those whom he thought would have the best chance of survival.

It was decided to keep the group small and select. We invited those individuals whom we could count on to be strong and loyal. They also needed to have certain skill set that would come in handy. All in all, we gathered up seven families with a total of thirty six people. We had four men with construction backgrounds, three hunters, two farmers, one doctor, and one cook. The women were equally talented. We had two with teaching skills, two nurses, one cook, one angler, and one seamstress. Five of the men and two of the women also had prior military experience. The children all ranged from eighteen down to four with seven girls and fourteen boys. The one common thread between all these families was that all the boys were boy scouts.

Four weeks of hurried preparations and secret meetings. It was during those meetings that everything was decided on what to bring and what not to bring. They chose what hand tools they would need and what kind of seeds to bring. They chose which clothes and shoes to bring. They selected specific books and manuals that they thought they would need. They discussed what else they should bring. How much food and what types to pack. They also packed other useful items like rope, tarps, fire starters, cooking supplies. Everybody made suggestions on what to bring and what not to bring. Everyone was well aware that everything that they brought, they would have to carry to wherever they were going. They made lists and checked them twice. They knew that there was no return. Then, they packed. Most of them packed their cars in secret. Many did it inside the garage with the door down. And as they packed their cars, they prayed. They prayed that all this was for nothing and that the whole scenario would not come to pass.

On the morning of Sept. 11, the air was filled with the sounds of gunfire. Sporadic at first, it soon grew in frequency and intensity. Everyone met in the church parking lot. The families were divided into separate cars to minimize the risk to any one family. Everyone had armed themselves with weapons for protection but most were not sure that they could actually take a life. The wives were assigned the duty of driving while the men and the oldest boys were assigned the job of protection. Their task was simple. Shoot if needed but shoot to kill. There was no mistaking the simple fact that their very lives were in the balance.

"John, their stopping the cars at the end of the street."

"Go around them, for God's sake, don't stop.

Floor it now!

Everyone, follow our lead."

Susan pressed hard on the accelerator of the truck. As the truck lurched forward, the rest of the vehicles followed. The big F-350 hit the front of the car blocking the road, throwing it into two other cars and opening up a path for the group to escape through.

The next few moments were filled with gunfire as seven trucks and cars went speeding through the one thing preventing their escape, the road block. The people gave chase as the group sped away to freedom. The chase lasted about a half a mile until John shot out the radiator of their pursuers cars with his shotgun. The group drove another half mile up the road and stopped just over the crest to check for damage. Mike took his hunting rifle and shot down on the group of thugs who were running up the road.

"We need to get going. They're still chasing us on foot."

Mike fired a second round and two thugs fell to the ground.

"Anyone hurt?"

"John, come quick. It's Mary. She's hurt pretty bad."

By the time John got to Mary, they had moved her to the ground next to the car.

"John, did we make it?"

"Yeah honey, we made it out safe."

"Is everyone OK?"

"Yeah."

I love you were the last words that Mary said to John before she died.

"Keep the kids away. I don't want them to see their mom like this."

John got up from the ground and grabbed his rifle. He walked to the crest of the hill, took careful aim and fired. One of the pursuers dropped to the ground dead. He chambered another round, took aim and pulled the trigger. Another one fell to the ground. The rest of the attackers stopped their pursuit. As John chambered a third round, Tom walked up.

"You can't get all of them."

"I can sure as hell try."

"John, this won't bring Mary back. Besides, we need you alive. You're the only one who knows where this place is and if you die now, then Mary died for nothing."

John took careful aim and fired a third time killing yet another one.

"That's for my wife, you Bastards."

They wrapped Mary in a blanket and laid her in the back of one of the trucks.

"Anyone else hurt?"

"We have four others with minor wounds. Nothing serious."

"Let's get moving, we've got a long drive ahead of us and an even longer walk."

John placed a blanket in the driver's seat of Mary's car and then got behind the wheel. John led the caravan down the road for several hours until they came to a two track which headed off into the woods.

"Turn here."

Seven vehicles made the turn into the woods and then stopped. John got out of his car and walked back to the road. There, he took a large leaf covered branch and started brushing away the tire tracks. He then dragged an old dead pine tree across the trail as if it had fallen there naturally.

"Someone would have to know that the trail was even here to find us." He mumbled to himself. They followed the trail for several miles until they came to the old bridge which crossed a mountain stream.

At the old bridge, they parked the cars in the woods so as not to be readily seen by anyone coming up the trail and then tried to hide them by covering them with brush and trees.

John called his sons over

"Boys, mom didn't make it."

Johns two boys fell to the ground and burst into tears. He tried to console them but there were no words that could take away their grief. John held his own grief in, there just wasn't time right now. Too much was at stake to let go. He would grieve later, he told himself.

"Boys, grab some shovels and we'll lay mommy to rest over there by that little oak tree."

John hoped that by helping to bury their mother, the boys could find some sort of closure.

They dug a shallow grave close to the stream. They placed Mary carefully into it. Patrick picked some wild flowers and placed them in her hands which were carefully folded across her chest. Mary had a peaceful look on her face. If someone didn't know better, they would think she was peacefully sleeping.

"Bill, would you mind saying some prayers over her."

As the little group gathered around Mary, the stark reality of their dire situation began to sink in. They realized that their very lives stood in the balance of their successful escape.

"Dear Lord, please accept Mary into your arms and show her the grace she so richly deserves. Please help her sons Patrick and Joseph find solace in the fact that she died trying to protect them from harm. Please bless everyone hear and keep them safe from harm as we venture out into the wilderness to start a new life free from the wickedness which has consumed the Earth which you created. Amen."

Everyone took a handful of dirt and threw it into the grave as a way of saying goodbye. John and Patrick stayed behind and finished burying Mary after everyone else left.

Everything considered, from a military standpoint, their escape was a success. Only one casualty and four wounded. But from a personal point of view, it was very costly. Especially to John.

"From here, we go on foot. Grab everything you can carry and follow me. Stay in line and try not to disturb too much as you walk. We've got to get moving now."

When everyone was ready, they followed John as he walked into the woods next to the stream. It was slow going following the stream. There wasn't an actual trail to be followed and every so often, they walked in the stream so as to try to hide their trail. They walked for a week in the woods next to the stream that led them to this place of safety or so they hoped.

The walk should have only taken about two days to complete but with all things considered, they made pretty good time. It's a lot different leading thirty five people through the woods carrying everything they own. Trying to be quiet and not leave a trail to follow. All the while, having to care for four wounded people too. The children were real troopers. Not all of them fully understood what was happening to their little worlds but they all understood their very lives depended on them being quiet and leaving no trail behind.

CHAPTER 2

O N THE MORNING OF the seventh day, John seemed to be more careful in concealing their tracks than usual.

"Just a little bit further everyone."

They walked most of the morning and stopped for lunch around one.

"Dave, Take everyone up stream until you come to a ""Y"" in the stream. Follow the left fork which is the smaller stream and go until you come to a clearing. I'll meet you in the clearing.

Everyone, you will need to stay in the stream until we stop again. Dave knows the way."

"Where are you going?"

"I need to go back and cover our tracks."

Dave headed everyone up stream and John headed back down stream. After three hours of walking on slippery rocks, Dave led the group to a small clearing inside of a small canyon. An hour later, John caught up with the group in the clearing. They had already started a small fire and were tending to the wounded.

"Hey John, how did you know that this was here?"

"I found it several years ago. I followed a wounded elk up here. It's actually a box canyon with cliff walls. Only one way in and out. It's pretty big too. I think it goes back about another half mile. The stream is actually fed from a waterfall in the back of the canyon."

"Go ahead and make some dinner for the kids but keep the fire small."

"You can also set up the tents but we may decide to move them a little later so don't get too comfortable here just in case."

"Janet wants to know what we should do about water."

"If she wants, I can run down to the corner market and get some. Besides, this is pure mountain spring water just like Arrowhead."

The sarcasm although not fully appreciated, was taken as a sign by everybody that they were going to be OK.

"Tell Janet to boil the water if she feels that it's not safe to drink. We can set up a water purification station in the morning."

This was taken as good news, it meant that the group was staying. Tom, John, Dave, Bill, and Rob met in the corner of the clearing where they discussed the best place to post the guard for the night while the rest of the group busied themselves with settling down for the night.

"In the morning, we need to take a good look at this place to figure out the best way to set it up."

"Are we going to stay here for a while?"

"Yeah, We'll stay here until the world settles down or dies off."

There was a slow sigh of relief from the group as they came to realize that they had made it to safety. Everyone started setting up camp for the night. The group, for all practical purposes, looked like a regular boy scout outing there for the weekend. Had it not been for the sheer exhaustion, there might have even been some night games going on. As it was, everyone just slept after dinner was done.

In the morning, the camp slowly awoken to the smells of campfire and coffee. Several of the parents started making breakfast for everyone while others sat around the fire and blankly stared at the flames licking the logs, silently worrying about their safety without trying to outwardly show it to the children.

John spoke:

"Have the kids go explore this place but make sure they stay together. I don't want anything to happen. The parents will meet after breakfast to start prioritizing the work load that needs to be done."

"The first thing we need to do is build a wall at the opening of this canyon."

"Do you think a wall will really keep anyone out?"

"The wall won't keep people out, it will however give us the necessary time to arm ourselves in the event that we get discovered."

"So, we wall ourselves in? What if we need to get out?"

"We can have a gate and may I suggest that we put the gate over the stream."

"Why?"

"The area over the stream will be hard to fortify and so will the gate area. By making the stream the gate, we can minimize the weak points in the wall and the stream will camouflage our tracks coming and going."

"How tall should we build the wall?"

"I think eight feet should be tall enough. We could cut the poles ten feet long and bury them in the ground two feet. Then we could plant bushes in front of the wall to conceal it even more."

"What about shelter? We can't be expected to live in tents the whole time can we?"

"We can start with building a common house that can be used by everyone. We'll make it big enough to fit everyone inside for safety sake."

"Just what are we going to build these shelters with?"

"Our hands."

"Very funny."

"There are plenty of trees and rocks around here. We'll just have to do it like the old days, before there were lumber stores and contractors to do it for us."

"Another problem we have is food. We didn't bring enough food to stay here forever. We left most of the food in the cars when we started walking."

"We will make do with what we have and what we can gather from the forest."

"Rob, after the meeting, go get us some meat for dinner. Just remember, one shot, one kill. No sense in giving away our location if we don't have to."

"Deer or elk?"

"Deer would be fine but elk would keep us in meat for several days."

"You don't expect us to eat wild animals, do you?"

"Where do you think your steaks come from?"

"Walmart, of course."

"Once we get everyone settled, some of us will go back to the cars to get the rest of the supplies. I just want to make sure it's safe first."

"Before we break up this meeting, I would like everyone to come up with some sort of layout for our community. Just remember that we will need garden space."

"I would like to meet again tomorrow. Take the rest of the day today and recuperate. We could all use a little down time."

The following morning, the entire group gathered around the fire for breakfast.

"Well kids, what did you discover yesterday?"

"This place is huge."

"Yeah, we must have walked for miles to find the end."

"There's even a waterfall at the end."

"And I saw some rabbits and a raccoon."

"And there's rocks everywhere."

"And lots of trees."

"There was even a couple of caves but I was too scared to go inside."

"One of the caves is right over there."

The child pointed to an area just behind the gathering.

"I saw a bunch of bees flying out of an old dead tree trunk."

"That's great kids."

The canyon, from what John remembered, was a box canyon. The opening to the canyon was just under fifty feet wide with most of it blocked by the pine trees. Once through the opening, the canyon opened up to about as wide as the length of a football field. The sides of the canyon were shear rock faces on the upper halves and piled up stones on the bottom halves. At the back of the canyon was a small waterfall about 40 feet in height. The water fell into a pool that was roughly thirty feet round before it meandered down the valley in a three foot wide stream. There were a great deal of pine trees of all sizes in the valley with most of them being along the walls of the canyon. There was a good size meadow that had a gentle slope to it which would make a fine garden area. Then there were the caves. One cave in the rear of the canyon looked to be dug by miners at one time. There was a lot of stone debris near the entrance. Perhaps, someone was looking for gold at some point. The second cave was near where John's group had decided to make camp. This cave was a natural cave that went back for about thirty feet before it stopped. It appeared that some ancient cave in sealed off the rest of the cave for good. This was the cave that Bob thought would make a good storage area for the food.

Over the next couple of days, the group busied themselves with layout and setup of their new community. They decided to put the sleeping quarters along both sides of the canyon. That way, the early birds could have the morning sun and the night owls would get the evening sun. The stream cut through the canyon more toward one side than the other. Everyone was given certain tasks to complete according to their age and skills. Most of the adults worked on the most pressing things first, like the wall. They were either cutting down the trees or digging the trench. They dug down two feet and cut the trees to ten feet. That way, the finished wall would be eight feet high. Too high to run and jump to get over. All the rocks that were dug up were put along the inside of the wall to further strengthen it. It would also provide someplace to look over the wall once it was finished. They lashed the tree trunks together one at a time and then tied more trees horizontally to give the wall the strength it needed. They made the gate as wide as the stream which was about three feet. They decided on a single gate with leather hinges. Once the wall was finished, they planted shrubs and native bushes to try to camouflage it from the outside.

Nothing was wasted. The branches from the trees were cut up into firewood for cooking and keeping warm at night. The extra stones were piled up to be used for the buildings.

Susan thought it would be a wise idea to build a dam so that there would be a better supply of water. Everyone was put to work. The youngest gathered up firewood and stacked it neatly in a pile (with parental support of course). The older ones picked up rocks out of the meadow and piled them on either side of the canyon. Mike started to put in a garden to try to get some fresh vegetables yet this year. This was a task in itself because the soil was a clay based soil and it stuck to the shovel every time they dug into it. Tom, Bill, Dave, and some of the oldest boys worked on building a solid dam across the stream to increase the water supply and to give a way across the stream without getting wet.

CHAPTER 3

O NCE THE FENCE WAS completed, the group started on the layout of the compound. The common house was designed as a long but almost narrow structure. It was about twenty feet wide and almost forty feet long. The walls were a mere six feet tall with the peak of the roof at eight feet. They placed the fireplace in the rear of the structure and several windows along either wall up close to the roof line. They made the walls out of stone which was very plentiful. They stacked the stones on top of one another and filled the gaps with smaller stones. Then they took the soil and mixed it with water and ashes from the fire. This mixture was then smashed into the crevices and cracks between the stones. This final step was given to the youngest of the children. They enjoyed helping out and they thought they were making mud pies. The roof was made from wood and tarps. They placed several trees along the ridge of the roof which they supported with posts on the inside. They then cut smaller trees that went from the top of the roof down to the side walls. They covered the entire roof with several tarps to make it waterproof. Finally, they covered the entire roof with dirt which was dug up while enlarging the pond. This gave a nice insulating factor to the house so that it would not be so hard to keep warm in the winter. The fireplace in the back was also made this way with the entire chimney being made from stone.

They placed the common house close to the near cave. They wanted to make the cave a food storage. They used the mud mixture on the back of the cave to seal out any little critters that might be hiding in the rocks.

Then, they built a wall at the entrance of the cave with a small opening for a door. This opening, they covered with one of the animal hides.

They next built a cooking area very similar to a large grill. It consisted of three small walls to concentrate the heat with the back wall being much taller than the rest. They placed the back wall facing the fence to shield the flames from being seen by anyone outside. They were able to use one of the flat stones as a door to a make shift oven.

Once the common house was done, the individual family units started on their own houses. Most were built as much smaller versions of the common house. It was decided that they should be for sleeping only. This would minimize the amount of materials that each house used. Some of the houses were built as duplexes with them sharing a common wall. Others were built as solo houses. They tried to keep some distance between each of the houses so that there was a little privacy. All of the houses had their own fireplaces for warmth. They used the tanned hides from the many deer that were shot as door coverings and window coverings. This allowed access into the houses while keeping most of the heat from the fireplace inside. It also gave each family a little privacy once inside their sleeping quarters.

When all the houses were completed, there were four houses on the east side of the canyon and three houses and the common house on the west.

Mike was hard at work digging up the soil for the garden. He knew that the garden would need to be pretty big to feed all thirty five people. He placed the garden more on the west side of the canyon. That way, it would get the morning and noon sun but would not get too much sun. mike knew that the soil would stay warm in the afternoon even without the sun shining directly on it. Digging the actual plot was very time consuming. It consisted of turning the soil by hand using the shovels and removing the rocks. Every shovel full of dirt would stick to the shovels and mike would have to use his foot to dislodge the dirt from his shovel. Mike did have the small child work force. The kids would help by removing the rocks that Mike dug up and taking them over to the house builders. The kids would also break up the larger clumps of dirt.

"How's it going there Mike?"

"To tell you the truth John, this soil is about the toughest stuff I ever ran into. It sticks to everything."

"What if you mixed sand in with it? Would that make it easier to till the next time?"

"Yeah, that would make a big difference but where are we going to get sand from? Everything here is clay."

"Check up at the waterfall. I'm pretty sure there's sand up there that got washed down the stream. Maybe there's some sand along the walls in those rubble piles."

"I think that will work. I can have the little ones gather the sand and dump it in the garden. They can make a game of it."

Mike had the smaller children start to gather the sand and dump it into the garden. He worked the sand into the clay soil as he turned the soil over. This made it easier to break up. Mike had his son and daughter helping him. It took the three of them about a week to clear a spot 30 X 50 and an additional 3 days to get the soil ready for planting. They planted a select variety of seeds at first. Plants that they knew would grow quickly. Radishes, lettuce, carrots. They even planted a few potatoes as a test.

The wall and common house took several weeks to complete. The community kitchen and storage cave were also completed in that time.

once the walls and homes were completed, Tom led a group of the larger boys back down to the cars to retrieve the rest of the food and whatever else they thought they might need.

"Tom, do you got everything you need?"

"Yes John, I have the list from Janet, all the keys to the cars, four backpacks and eight duffel."

"If you see anything suspicious or think it's not safe, leave the stuff there. Your safety is more important than anything that might be in the cars."

"John, I'll see you in four days. No worries."

Tom led the group out the gate with quiet reservations. He didn't want to let on that he was just a little scared. He carried with him two pistols and a rifle just in case. The boys, all eagle scouts, fully understood the gravity of the situation and the mission they were embarking on. Four days in the woods without leaving a trail and without being spotted by anything or any one.

On the evening of the fourth day, Tom returned with everything he was instructed to get.

"How did it go?"

"I told you John, no worries. We didn't see or hear anything out of the ordinary. However, down by the cars, there was the smell of smoke and there was an eerie glow in the western sky long after sunset. If I had to guess, I would say the whole city was on fire."

"That doesn't surprise me. Our whole world has gone up in smoke. We were just lucky enough to get out in one piece."

Tom and the boys took the food they brought and placed it in the storage cave. With careful planning and supplementing with food gathering and hunting, they figured there should be enough to last until harvest time.

It only took a little while until everything fell into a routine. Every couple of days, Rob would leave the compound in the morning and return with enough meat to last a little while. Mike tended the garden to make sure the plants produced. Tom and Bill worked on the houses doing the final touches to make them weather tight. Dave and John cut firewood to stock up for the winter. The younger children started attending school in the common house. Some of the ladies were mending clothes and making curtains from the animal skins. The older children gathered nuts and berries from the back of the canyon. They also carried water from the stream to water the garden.

CHAPTER 4

"**M**OMMY, THIS WAY. I hear voices."
"Be careful son, we don't know who it might be."
"Look mom, there's a wall here by the stream."
The sentries heard the family coming through the woods. They were following the stream in the directions of the noises. Not wanting to shoot if they didn't have to, the sentries took careful aim at the family as they approached the wall. When the family was in the little clearing, the sentry spoke.
"Halt."
"Go get John."
One of the younger kids went running to John.
"John, there's someone at the gate."
John walked quickly to the gate. He opened up the gate long enough for him to slip through the opening and the gate closed behind him with click of the lock.
"May I help you?"
"Yes" there was a sigh of relief." My name is Martha Jones and we need your help. We were stopped by some armed men. They pulled us out of the car and walked us out into the woods. They were going to kill us."
"What were you doing driving out here anyway?"
"We were trying to reach our family in California. We haven't heard from them since all this trouble started and we needed to find them."
"May we come in?"

"I'm sorry but I'm not authorized to let you in. only the council has that authority."

"May I speak with them?"

"They have been notified of your presence here and they will come talk to you shortly. In the meantime, can I get you some food and water?"

"Yes, that would be great."

"Guard, send Patrick out."

Patrick will take your daughter inside and they will get you some food. It isn't much, but it's all we have to offer.

"My daughter isn't going in there. Not without all of us."

"If you are concerned of her safety, I give you my word of honor that nothing will happen to her. However, if you would rather go without, that would be fine too. It's up to you."

"Please mommy, I'll be OK. I'm really hungry."

Patrick came out of the gate.

"Yes father?"

"Patrick, take this girl inside and get some food for the family."

"Hi, my name is Patrick. Come on."

"Please mommy? I'll be OK."

"OK. I want your promise that she will be OK"

"I promise you that no harm will come to your daughter."

Patrick took the girl in through the gate and appeared a short time later with a gallon of water and a pot of venison stew.

"Patrick, set up a small fire for them to keep warm, it'll get cold tonight."

"Yes father."

As they finished their stew, the council approached the family.

"John, what do we have here?"

"Gentlemen, this is Martha Jones and her two children. They found us and are requesting to join our community."

The council consisted of five of the adults. They were elected to the council by the rest of the group. The council has final say about everything that happens in the community. Nothing of importance ever happens without the council's approval.

Martha knew at once that she would need to present her case eloquently and passionately if she hoped to be allowed to stay.

"Gentlemen, I humbly ask your permission to stay and join your group."

"Martha, start from the beginning and tell us everything that happened."

"Well", Martha started, "we hadn't heard from Dukes parents, that's my husband, since this all began. So, we decided to drive the back roads to California to reach his parents. We needed to sneak in and bring them back to the Midwest where they would be safe."

Martha explained how they were stopped by a group of armed men two days ago. They were going to kill the family. Two of them took the whole family out into the woods to shoot them.

One of the men put down his gun and was going to rape Martha. That's when Duke grabbed the other man and hit him, knocking him down. He told Martha to run so Martha and the kids ran into the woods. The first man reached for his gun and killed Duke. Martha ran through the woods with the men shooting at them and they fell down a big hill and landed in a stream. Martha grabbed the kids and ran down the stream. She could hear the men shouting and swearing at them as they disappeared into the forest.

"That was two days ago and we have been following the stream this whole time."

"Did the men follow you down the hill?"

"No, after about an hour, I couldn't hear their voices anymore. If they had followed us, they would have found us by now."

"You may sleep out here tonight. Tomorrow, we'll give you our decision."

Martha stood there feeling completely helpless. Tears started welling up in her eyes but she fought to hold them off. At least until the council left. She didn't want them to see her break down.

While Martha was recanting what had happened over the past two days. Patrick was busy setting up a small fire for the family.

"Martha", said John, "keep the fire small. We don't want it to be a beacon for the whole world to see."

With that, the whole group went back inside the gate and locked it. Only the sentries were there watching out over the little family.

"What do you think, John?"

"I think it's not my decision to make. I'm only here to enforce what you decide."

"You have no opinion about this?"

"My opinion doesn't matter."

The council retired to the main house to start discussing what they should do.

"Dad?"

"Yes Patrick."

"What do you think will happen to them?"

"I don't know."

"You think they will get cold tonight?"

"They have a small fire to keep warm."

"I'm worried about those kids. They seem like nice kids and I'd hate to see anything happen to them."

"What do you want to do?"

"Can I give them my blanket?"

"That means you go without."

"I have more. Besides, I don't want them to get cold." stated Patrick.

"If you want to give them your blanket, I'll allow it."

John had the guard open the gate long enough for Patrick to take his blanket to the family.

"Here, this will help keep you warm tonight."

"Thank you. Martha said."

As Patrick turned to go back, Martha wrapped the blanket around her two children. Then she put another piece of wood on the fire. She watched as the embers floated up into the sky like a hundred lightening bugs flying up to heaven. As she watched, she prayed. She prayed that the community would accept her and her family.

"That was very nice of you Patrick."

"I just wish there was something more I could do."

"Like what?"

"Could I talk to the council?"

"I don't know. Do you think that would be wise?"

"Please dad?"

"OK"

John and Patrick walked to the common house in silence. Everyone was talking about the same thing but Patrick didn't really hear them. It was all a mumble in his ears. As they approached the door, they could hear the council talking but they couldn't make out the words.

"Patrick," said John, "remember that they are the rule makers. What they say is final. Treat them with respect and look them in the eyes when you are talking to them. Speak clearly and slowly."

"Yes dad, I know."

Patrick knocked on the door and waited. He waited for them to recognize him and invite him in.

"come in."

Patrick opened the door and stepped through it. The door closed quietly behind him. He stood there for a moment, letting his eyes adjust to the dim light. He then walked and stood in front of the council.

"How may we help you today Patrick?"

"Has a decision been made about the family yet?"

"Not yet."

"I would like to speak on behalf of the family if I may."

"Please go ahead and speak."

Patrick stood there, looking at each one of them in the eyes. He took a deep breath.

"Gentlemen, I think that the family should be allowed to stay."

"Why?"

"I think that if we send the family away, they will die out there in the forest or worse, get killed by someone."

"Patrick, we don't have a lot of food to just take anyone in who shows up. If they stay, it will mean more work for everyone."

"They can help."

"But what if they don't know how to do anything?"

"We can teach them. Wasn't it the council who said that many hands make light work?" I don't want the kids to die just because their parents didn't teach them how to work. After all they need our help and isn't that the Christian thing to do? Help those less fortunate than ourselves?"

"Are there any other reasons why you want them to stay?"

"What do you mean?"

"Any personal reasons?"

"Like what?"

"Like maybe you like them, or at least the girl?"

Patrick started to blush. A small grin began to creep across his face. "Maybe."

"Is there anything else you wish to discuss with us?"

"No."

"You may be excused, Patrick."

Patrick turned around and started walking out of the room. At the doorway, paused, turned again to face the council.

"Thank you for allowing me the opportunity to speak to you."

With that, Patrick turned again and left the building letting the door close quietly behind him.

"How did it go?" asked John.

"Fine. Dad, do you think they will let them stay?"

"I don't know Patrick. You should be very proud of yourself. It takes a lot of courage to address the council."

"Thanks dad."

"Off to bed, you still have your chores that need to be done."

In the morning, Patrick was the first one up. He quickly got dressed and went to make a breakfast for the guests outside the fence. As he opened the gate, he could see the family huddled together, all wrapped in his blanket. The last few embers of the fire still glowing in the fire pit. He put down the breakfast next to the family and started to make a new fire. After a few moments, there was a small fire starting again. The flames, licking the fresh wood.

The crackling of the fire woke Martha first. She quickly glanced at the breakfast and then at Patrick.

"Did you bring us breakfast?"

"Yes ma'am."

"And you started the fire too. Thank you. Thank you for everything."

"I need to get going. I still have a lot of chores to do today."

With that, Patrick went back inside the gate.

As they were finishing their breakfast, the council emerged from the gate and approached Martha.

"Martha, we have made a decision."

Martha stood and faced the council. She tried not to show any fear in front of her children but it was written across her face. The council, seeing her stand and face them took it as a good sign that they made the right decision.

"Martha, do you agree to follow the rules of this community no matter what the personal consequences are?"

"We will follow the rules to the best of our ability."

"With that said, you and your family may stay. Welcome to our community."

A wave of relief rushed over Martha. Her face became red and her knees got weak. She started to cry.

"Mommy, are you OK?"

"Yes baby, I'm OK. We're all going to be OK."

As the council, turned to leave, Mike spotted Patrick's blanket. He gave John a questioning look but John just returned the look with a knowing nod. They extinguished the little fire and everyone walked into the gate.

CHAPTER 5

W HEN MARTHA ENTERED THE compound, she could hardly believe her eyes. There was a fairly large building built off to the one side. In front of that was a stone cooking area where the food was prepared. In the center of the compound was a large garden area with plants growing in nice rows. The stream which flowed through the gate was dammed up to create a small pond. All along the sides of the compound were smaller buildings in various stages of completion. Some were almost done while others were just foundations. Everyone was busy working on something. Even the very young were gathering firewood and stacking it in a pile.

"See mommy, I told you there were a lot of people here."

"You were right honey, there is a lot of people here."

Martha saw Patrick standing in the pond digging up rocks from the bottom and putting them on shore. She waved to him and he got a big smile on his face and waved back.

"Hi Patrick!"

"How long has your group been here." Asked Martha

"We arrived about six weeks ago. We knew of this location and decided that this would be our best chance at survival. We packed up and left the morning the trouble started."

"Martha," called the council, "we need to set down the ground rules for you. Everyone here has agreed to follow these."

Martha follow the council into the common building along with her children. Once inside, they sat in a circle on some hand made chairs.

"First, do you have any special talents that we should know about?"

"Like what?" Asked Martha.

"Anything that you feel might be beneficial to the community."

"I was a teachers aid and I can sew."

"Anything else?"

"Not that I can think of."

"We can always use another teacher. One of the requirements is that the children attend classes. We feel education is very important but we only teach them the basics for obvious reasons."

"OK, we can live with that."

"Rule number one. The good of the community comes before the good of the individual.

Rule number two. You will have to become self sufficient meaning you need to do your own work.

Rule three. The council makes all the decisions concerning the welfare of the community.

Do you agree with these rules."

"Yes."

"Very well. Do you have any questions?"

"Where will my family sleep?"

"You can sleep in here for now until you get your house built. There are several families who still sleep in here. It will be a little crowded but it will keep you dry and safe."

"I have to build my own house?"

"Yes, everyone builds their own house."

"But I don't know how."

"Don't worry, we will help you with it but part of becoming self sufficient is stuff like that. Besides, it will give you a sense of accomplishment and pride in the end. Trust us on this, we know what we're talking about."

"Are there fish in the pond? I love fishing."

"Not yet but we hope to start raising some soon. That's why Patrick is digging out the rocks from the bottom of the pond. We need to make it deeper so that the fish will survive the winter."

"You know what, we passed some apple trees a day before we found your camp."

"Would you mind showing us the way? That would go a long way in supplementing our food."

"I would be happy to show you."

The next day, John, Bob, and Martha set out with some empty containers and a shovel to find apples.

As the trio walked quietly through the woods, they discovered through Martha that the killing was not as extensive back East as it was here in the West. Martha's husband had been a banker in Chicago with one of the big banks and they had a condo overlooking Lake Michigan. Her children, Sally and Gary were average children. Sally was just starting Girl Scouts, she played the piano, was good at math, and enjoyed helping Martha in the kitchen. Gary was a cub scout, played soccer and football, enjoyed school (especially recess), liked to fish. It was mostly Martha and Bob doing the talking. John was half listening to their conversation. He was more intent on listening to mother nature for any sounds that didn't belong. John was also observing the terrain and the stream. He was looking for pools of water where fish might be. He knew that once the pond was dug out, they would need to stock it.

"The trees were over this way. I remember Sally left the stream and walked into the woods to go potty. When she came back, she was eating an apple."

They left the stream side and walked into the woods about twenty feet. There in front of them were three large apple trees full of fruit along with several small saplings.

"This is great! Look at all the fruit on these trees."

"This is wonderful. Lets get these packs full so maybe we can get back while it's still light."

Everyone worked fast to fill all the containers, three backpacks and three duffel bags. John then started digging up some of the saplings and wrapping their root balls with cloth.

"That's what you brought the shovel for. Exclaimed Martha."

"Yes ma'am, this was what I was hoping to find. A future orchard for inside our compound. Martha, would you mind carrying the shovel back to camp?"

"I would be happy to."

They started back to camp fully loaded. Martha had her backpack, duffel and the shovel. Bob and John each had their backpacks and duffel s and two saplings. The trio walked back into camp as the sun was beginning to paint the skies with reds, orange, and purples.

"Everyone, come get a nice treat!"

Everybody came and took several apples to enjoy. How long has it been since they had fresh fruit was anybody's guess. They put most of the apples into the storage area where it was a lot cooler.

John went and planted the four saplings along the west side of the canyon. That way, they would receive the morning sun which would help them grow.

It was a cool, brisk morning. Winter was trying to show her ugly head and everyone agreed that it was too early for her to show up. The morning breeze had changed direction from the previous night.

"I think we need to change the location of the outhouse" said Jill.

"Why? That would mean a lot of work. The hole is deep enough to last all winter."

"Don't you smell it? It's ruining my appetite for breakfast."

"That smell isn't from the outhouse" said John.

John was raised in the country and he hadn't smelled anything like that since childhood. The farm next to John's childhood home raised chickens and cows and the smell being carried into camp on the morning breeze was a combination of chicken and cow manure.

"I think I'll go for a walk this morning" said John.

"Want some company?" Said Tom

"sure."

"Looking for anything in particular John?"

"Not really."

"If you find a store," said Jill, "would you mind getting some bacon and eggs for breakfast. I'm getting tired of venison stew for every meal."

"Anything else, said John jokingly."

"Coffee would be nice."

"I'll see what I can do." Said John.

CHAPTER 6

A FTER BREAKFAST, JOHN AND Tom headed out. John knew that there had to be a farm close by for the smell to be that strong. The two followed the scent for several miles until they came to the edge of a clearing. There on the far side of the clearing was the source of the smells. It was a' small farmhouse with several barns. There were about 30 cows in the clearing all confined behind barbed wire. From one of the barns, the sounds of chickens could be heard. There was a pig pen with several sows and piglets in it. They could see smoke coming from the chimney on the house. Someone was home. They approached slowly and cautiously so as not to make any movements visible from the house. Tom and John waited to see if they could determine who might be there and if they might be friendly.

"Tom, you stay here. I'm going to sneak around to the back of the house and look inside. I'll signal you if it's safe."

"What if something happens to you?"

"Make your way back to camp and tell them what happened."

John made his way carefully around to the back of the house. As he peered in the back window, he looked straight into the business end of a shotgun.

"Hold it right there. Who are you and what are you doing on my farm?" The voice sounded as if it hadn't slept for years.

"Don't shoot mister. I mean you no harm. My name is John."

"What are you doing here."

"I came looking for supplies. I followed the scent of the cows here."

The man lowered the shotgun and motioned for John to open the door and come in.

John carefully opened the door to the house and cautiously stepped inside. John stood there for a moment carefully surveying the area. He was standing in the back foyer just off the kitchen. There were shelves to his left which were about half full of canned goods and other food items. To his right was the wall which had a dozen coat hooks evenly spaced along it with several of the hooks holding winter coats. Just past the foyer was the kitchen which was complete with table and chairs.

"Come on in here."

"Yes sir," spoke John.

"No need to call me sir, my name is George Goodwell."

"George, my name John."

"Well john, what brings you to my back door?"

"To tell you the truth, by now you know what's been happening in the world lately."

"Yeah, I saw the news. It's a real shame that people can't just get along. Now they have to go and kill each other and for what? Because of the color of their skin? That's just plain stupidity."

"Well, myself and a group of others escaped the morning it all hit the fan and we've been hiding up here to try to stay safe."

"Where you all at?"

"I would rather not say. Not that I don't trust you but if you don't know where we are, you can't be forced to tell."

"I know what you mean but let me tell you, I served in the army during Korean and Vietnam. I was a P.O.W. in Korea. The Koreans couldn't make me talk. I seriously doubt that these people can do it but I respect you wanting to look out for the others. Is there anything I can get you?"

"Well, we could use some coffee."

"We?"

"yes sir, my partner is still on the edge of the woods."

"Tell him to come on then and stop calling me sir."

"Sorry, it's a habit I picked up from the Marines."

"You were in?"

"86 to 92."

John got up from the table and walked to the back door. He went outside and motioned to Tom to come in. Tom walked to the house and stepped inside.

"George, this is Tom. Tom, this is George."

"How do you do."

George stood up and stuck his hand out in Tom's direction. Tom took hold of Georges hand and gave it a good firm shake.

"George, I believe you mentioned some coffee."

"Almost forgot. How do you take it?"

"Black" Both men said in unison.

They sat there and talked for almost an hour. Small talk mostly. Tom got the feeling that George was lonely for some company. George was getting up there in age and the house was showing signs of wear and neglect.

"George," said Tom, "do you have any family close by that checks up on you periodically?"

"No, it's just me here. The misses past away several years back and Nathaniel, that's my son, died over in Iraq."

"Is there any other family?"

"No, I was an orphan as a child so I don't know of any other family."

"Aren't you afraid being here all by yourself?"

"Son, I've lived a long time. I'm more afraid of living than of dying. Sometimes, I think God forgot I was down here."

"Trust me George," said John, "God hasn't forgotten about you. He just isn't finished with you yet."

"Is there anything you guys need out there in the woods?"

"There's a few things we lack but for the most part, we came pretty well prepared."

"If there's anything you need, please, help yourself. Take whatever you need."

"What about you George, anything you need?"

"I could use a little help with some repairs if you guys are handy at all."

"Tell us what you need and we'll take care of it if we can."

So the three of them worked out a little barter system. George needed some work done around the house to make his life a little easier and in return, John and Tom got some supplies that they still needed. John put up the storm windows and stacked the wood on the porch while Tom repaired the missing shingles on the roof. Then, they brought up food out of the basement and re stocked the pantry, and fixed the leaking faucet in the bathroom. Finally, they stacked the bales of hay so that George could reach them easier. In return, they got several pounds of coffee, a pile of rope, some vegetable seeds, a new saw, another shovel and an ax.

"Is there anything else you need?"

"Well, Jill did want some bacon and eggs for breakfast."

"Eggs? I have a whole chicken coop full of eggs. Take as many as you want. They're just going to waste anyway."

"What about one of those piglets out there? Are they weened from their mother yet?"

"Sure, take several."

"No, just one will be fine."

"George," asked Tom, "how come you have so many egg producing chickens if it's just you?"

"I used to sell them down at Jackson's store. Made pretty good money too."

"What happened?"

"Well, just after all this trouble started, a group of them came to the store and robbed it. Old man Jackson put up a struggle so they shot him right there in his own store. Then, they torched the place. Luckily, they ain't made it out here yet."

"You sure you don't want to come back with us?"

"No. Like I said before, death don't scare me."

"Well, if it's alright with you, I'd like to come back sometime just to check up you."

"Fine, fine. You just come on back when you get some time."

"Good luck George. You be safe here."

"You all be safe out there too."

Tom and John wound up taking six dozen eggs and a piglet along with everything else. They tied a rope around the piglet and led it into the woods with the piglet fighting and squealing the whole way.

"Why did you want the pig?"

"Jill said she wanted some bacon. Besides, we can feed it all the leftover food scraps that Mike wants to compost and come springtime, we can slaughter it for the meat.

We'll have to make a pen for it."

"Just don't let the kids name the pig."

"Why?"

"If they name it, we'll never be able to eat it."

"Good point."

The two made it back to camp close to suppertime.

"Jill," said Tom, "we stopped at the store on the way back and picked up some things for you."

"What did you guys get for me this time?"

"Breakfast."

Tom handed Jill the duffel full of eggs and John gave her the rope tied to the pig.

"You asked for eggs and bacon for breakfast. We even managed to gather some coffee and other supplies."

John gave the seeds to Mike for the garden and put the rest of the supplies in the common house.

"Where did you get this stuff?" Asked Jill.

"Did you steal it from someone?"

"No, we traded for it." Said Tom.

"From who?"

John said "some things are better off not knowing"

john's statement put an end to any other questions. The group knew that John did not want to tell them too much for their own protection.

The next morning, everyone enjoyed fresh eggs and venison steak for breakfast along with the delicious cup of coffee.

"You know what would go really well with this coffee?"

"What?"

"Some sweetener."

"I'm sweet. Let me put my fingers in your coffee. That should make it taste much better."

"Very funny."

"We brought back some sugar, didn't we?"

"We're saving that for cooking."

"What about some honey?" Said Joe.

"What honey?"

"Honey from that dead tree back in the canyon."

John had forgotten about the children finding the dead tree with all the bees when they first arrived.

"We can go look and see."

CHAPTER 7

T HEY MADE PLANS ON how best to retrieve any honey that might be inside the tree. Mike devised a make shift bee suit out of a long sleeve shirt, long pants and some netting. They tied the bottom of the pant legs to the tops on Mike's boots and they tied his shirt sleeves to his gloves. They placed some old screen from one of the damaged tents loosely around his head and put a hat on his head to hold the netting in place. Next, they attached the net to his shirt collar. As a final act, they had Mike stand in the smoke from the fire to mask his "human" smell.

"You ready?"

"As ready as I'll ever be. We need some containers to put the honey in and some rope to fix the tree when we're done."

Mike and Tom headed up the canyon with everything they needed. When they reached the tree, the morning sun was just over the canyon rim enough to just caress the top of the tree. The tree itself was little more than a standing stump, maybe seven feet tall and three feet round. There was an opening at the bottom of the tree and the entire top was open to the sky. The rest of the tree was laying on the ground, the victim of a lightning strike or maybe a strong wind.

Mike took some dried leaves and grass and placed them inside the opening at the bottom of the tree and he lit it. The grass caught fire and produced an abundance of smoke which rose up through the middle of the tree and escaped out the top. The sight looked like a chimney from a house. Once the bees stopped flying around, Mike went to work on opening the tree and exposing the hive. He removed a section of the tree to reveal several nice honey combs inside, stacked like little shelves. Mike carefully removed each honey comb. He used his knife to scrape the wax off one side of the comb which allowed the honey to flow. He poured the honey from the comb into the containers. When the honey was removed, he carefully replaced the comb back into its original location and started on the next one. There was enough honey to fill all the containers that they brought along.

"Should we keep the wax too?"

"Sure, we can find a use for it somewhere."

Once they finished collecting the honey, Mike carefully placed the section of tree that he removed, back into position.

"Hand me the rope."

"Why?"

"I want to secure this piece of the tree so that the bees will make more honey for us this spring."

Mike and Tom headed back to camp with three containers of honey and two softball size clumps of bees wax.

"Mike, how did you learn to do that?"

"Easy, my grandfather used to be a bee keeper in the mid-west. He used to take his bees out into the orchards to pollinate the fruit trees. The other farmers actually paid him for it because it would increase their harvest. I also watched the pest control people in town when they had to remove a hive from someone's home."

"I hope the honey will keep for a while. I don't want to have to repeat this process any time soon."

"Have no fear, the honey will keep very well. They say that when the Pharoahs tombs were opened, they found some vessels of honey. It had crystalized but it was still good. All they did was heat it up and it became liquid again."

When Mike and Tom returned to camp, Jill was just finishing up the breakfast dishes.

"Here is some sweetener for your coffee."

"Thank you very much."

Tom put most of the honey inside the storage cave for safe keeping. Tom noticed that the storage area was getting a little chaotic inside.

"Mike, I think we need to make some baskets or something to hold all the supplies in storage. Especially, once we harvest the garden. Maybe, I should have woodworking class make some baskets."

"That would be a wonderful idea."

Tom set to work on getting the class to making baskets. He showed the students how to weave saplings and small branches into baskets of different sizes. Each basket was taking several hours to make. In all, the class made over twenty baskets for the storage cave.

CHAPTER 8

"**D**AD, WAKE UP!"
"What is it Joe."
"It snowed last night."

John got out of bed, put on his clothes and walked out the door of his house. There was a white blanket of snow several inches thick covering everything in the camp. There were smoke trails coming from several of the house chimneys. The stream was flowing into the pond creating small waves which were accentuated by the thin layer of shush floating on top. As the slush was pushed closer to the dam side of the pond, it began to thicken and solidify into a thin layer of ice. The sky was beginning to lighten to a deep blue. You could hear several birds singing in the trees toward the back of the canyon. It gave the entire area the look of a Norman Rockwell painting.

"Joe, better get a fire going in the kitchen. I think we're going to need lots of coffee this morning."

Joe did what he was told and started a fire in the grill. He then got several pots of water and started them heating up. The temperature really wasn't that cold, maybe thirty two degrees. John knew that most of the snow would be melted by noon but the garden was in danger of freezing out before it could produce any food.

"Good morning Mike. What a rude awakening this morning."

"I hope we didn't lose the garden last night."

"I don't think it frosted, just an early snow but we better figure out a way to protect the garden before it happens again."

The smell of coffee was slowly waking everyone up to a winter wonderland. One by one, the door flaps on the houses would open and then close again with the people finally coming out in their winter clothes.

"Mike, do you think the garden is gone?"

"I'm not sure Jill but we need to figure out something before this happens again."

Once everyone was awake, an impromptu meeting began with the main topic being on how to best protect the plants from the rapidly changing weather. Several suggestions were discussed such as building enclosures out of the extra tarps or bringing the plants inside the houses at night. It was decided that they would build low frames to support the tarps over the smaller plants and build enclosures to cover the larger plants.

"First thing we need is to have the kids remove the snow from the garden so that the sun can warm the ground again. Have the kids put the snow inside the storage cave. That should help to keep the food cold and make it last a little longer."

"Good idea mike. It's ashamed we don't have any green tarps to build the houses out of."

"Why's that John?"

"Well, we are building green houses aren't we?"

From somewhere behind them, a snowball hit John in the back of the head and slowly ran down the inside of his collar causing him to shiver with a sudden chill."

"That serves you right John for making stupid jokes."

"Gee Mike, I thought it was actually pretty clever."

By mid-day, all the snow was removed from the garden and the tarps were in place to help keep the ground warm as long as possible. There was also a renewed effort to gather up enough firewood for everyone at their houses.

"It's a good thing we had those extra supplies from George. Otherwise, we wouldn't have had enough to cover the whole garden."

"You're right Tom, it is a good thing. I wonder how George is faring these days?"

"Well John, there's only one way to find out."

"I know, maybe I'll take one of the boys with me this time. He seems to really enjoy having children around. Besides, they can do a little fishing in Georges pond so we can stock our pond some more."

Over the past few weeks, John had made several trips to check up on

George. He made pretend that the group needed things but he really just wanted to make sure that George was doing OK living by himself. Twice, he had taken one of the boys with him. John wanted his boys to learn that it was their duty as good Christians to take care of others. When Joe went, he did some of the chores but mostly, he entertained George with his guitar. When Patrick went, he caught some fish which they brought back with them to stock the pond. It was Joe's turn again to go. John gathered up the fishing pole and several five gallon buckets for the trip.

"Joe, we're going to go check on George tomorrow. Do you think you can catch some fish for the pond while we're there?"

"Sure dad, I'd love to go see George. I really like him."

"Good, we'll leave in the morning."

By next morning, all the snow was melted except what was covered by shade. John and Joe gathered up the buckets and poles along with two backpacks. They stepped into the stream and headed out through the gate.

"Can I go too?"

"No Patrick, you went last time. It's Joe's turn."

CHAPTER 9

T HEY HEARD THE GATE close behind them with the familiar locking of the door. The two of them walked in silence, listening to the sounds of nature and listening for the sounds of man. These trips were good for the boys. It taught them how to listen for what didn't belong. They carefully picked their way up stream, making very little noise. As they rounded one of the bends in the stream, they came upon a couple of deer with their backs to them, eating some of the forest grasses which grew along the banks. John froze in place and slowly pointed at the deer. Joe looked in the direction and the two just stood there and watched as the deer meandered away unaware of the human intruders.

"That was cool, Joe whispered to his dad once the deer left."

John just smiled at Joe and nodded his head in agreement. They continued on toward Georges house. As they approached the back of the fields, they began to sense that something was wrong. The cattle, which were usually up by the barn, were all in the back of the field but were looking toward the house.

"Joe, stay low. Something doesn't feel right."

"What is it dad?"

"Look at the cows, they should be up by the barn. It's feeding time."

"Dad, I hear voices but I can't understand the words."

"That's because they aren't speaking English."

The two of them crawled on their stomachs to the edge of the fence and looked toward the house. There were several people walking around the yard, going in and out of the barns. Others were going into the house and carrying stuff out and putting it into their cars. They seem to be gathering around one of the clothes line poles but John couldn't figure out why. John took the scope off his rifle and held the scope to his eye. Suddenly, he gasped.

"What did you see dad?"

John saw George tied Christ fashion to the post. He was naked and bloody. The group was slowly torturing George so that he would tell them where he hid his money. There was a familiar feeling of hatred welling up in John. If it wasn't for the fact that he had to worry about Joe, John would have put the scope back on the rifle and started firing.

"Dad?"

"They're torturing George."

"What?"

John handed the scope to Joe so that he could see what was going on. Joe put the scope to his eye. He watched as three men with knives were cutting George one at a time. They weren't deep cuts, but they bled a lot. The blood was running down Georges body making a crimson stain on the ground around his feet.

"Why would they do that? He's just a nice old man."

"I don't know Joe. The whole world has gone crazy. We better go before they find us out here."

Suddenly, there was a shot. John turned to look and saw Georges body go limp. There was a man with a pistol pointing it at Georges head.

"At least he's not suffering anymore."

The two of them crawled back down the hill, grabbed their stuff from where they left it and headed back to the stream. They walked back in silence. The only noise was the sniffling that Joe made as he tried to hold back his tears. As they got near the camp, John stopped and turned to Joe.

"Now, do you understand why we had to leave town and hide way up here?"

"Yes."

"Dad, why didn't you help George?"

"I couldn't risk it."

"Risk what?"

"Risk getting you hurt or worse. If you weren't with me, I would have tried to make them pay for what they did to George but I couldn't chance you getting hurt or captured. I had to consider your safety along with the security of the community. George understood the cost of living alone in these times and he accepted it fully. I only hope that you understand and appreciate his sacrifice."

"Do you think he told them about us?"

"George died protecting our secret. Do you understand why I couldn't help George?"

"Yes."

"Joe, I don't want you to speak of what you saw at Georges."

"Why?"

"It will just cause more hatred and that's what started this mess to begin with."

"But what do I say if anyone asks?"

"Just tell them that George went away."

"Do you think he went to Heaven?"

"I'm sure of it. He finally completed his task that God needed him to do."

They walked the rest of the way to camp. Once inside, Joe went straight to his house. Once inside, he curled up in his bed and cried.

"So how is old George?"

"Don't ask, Tom."

"What, he wasn't there?"

"He's gone."

The look in John's eyes told the story that his words tried to hide. The pain and anguish were written on his face. Tom saw that look, slowly nodded in understanding and walked away. No other words needed to be said.

John waited about a week before returning to George's house. As he cautiously approached the back of the pasture, he noticed the cows were busy grazing. He carefully scanned the entire area with his scope. There was no movement anywhere around the house and barns. There were no strange vehicles in the driveway and no movement in any of the windows of the house. John silently observed the entire area for over an hour before making his way along the perimeter of the property to the house. John cautiously made his way to the back porch as he did that first time. The lifeless body was still tied to the clothes line post with the hum of the flies filling John's ears.

John made a quick but thorough search of the house to make sure no one else was inside before grabbing a blanket and going outside to remove the body. John laid the blanket out at Georges feet. He then cut the ropes that bound him and lowered him to the waiting blanket. John wrapped the body in the blanket and carried it back into the house where he placed it in George's favorite chair.

John went to the pantry and gathered all the food he could carry. George always said to take anything we needed. Besides, George wouldn't need it anymore. Next, John went to the barn where he caught four hens and placed them inside a burlap bag. He opened the remaining cages and released the other hens so that they wouldn't starve to death. John also tied up the pregnant sow with a rope.

"Be free, there is no one left here to feed and water you"

John then went outside and opened the gate to the pasture so that the cows could be free. He went to the pen where the pigs were kept and opened the gate. He then gathered everything he had collected to take back to camp.

As John approached the house for the final time, he said a prayer to God "Dear Lord, please accept the soul of George into your arms. He was a decent man who gave of himself and asked for nothing in return". John lit a match and threw it into a pile of papers that were stacked behind the back door. John closed the back door behind him, gathered up his stuff and headed towards the back of the pasture. As he made his way through the fence, he looked back to see the entire house engulfed in flames. Even from this distance, John could feel the extreme heat of the fire on his face. It was a stark contrast from the brisk cold air of the coming winter.

John made his way back to camp being careful to erase any trail he might have left along the way.

CHAPTER 10

"M IKE?"
"Yes John."
"Do you think it's time to harvest the garden?"
"I want to let the squash grow as long as possible."
"I understand. I just don't want to lose everything to another snow. The cold snaps hit with very little warning. I think we prolonged the growing season as long as possible."
"Maybe you're right. No sense in tempting fate."
Mike gathered up the older children and began to harvest the garden. He taught them the best way to pick the vegetables so that they didn't get bruised. They harvested lots of zucchini, radishes, yellow squash, beets, acorn squash, and carrots. They even managed to get some lettuce which they ate right away.
"Be careful how you put these into storage. If you bruise them they will spoil very fast and cause the ones around them to spoil too."
Jill and some of the others were busy preserving the vegetables so that they would keep through the winter.
"Mike, let's take some of the tarps and make an actual greenhouse. Maybe, we could get a jump on the growing season next year or even get two crops."
"John, that sounds like a brilliant idea. I could use it as sort of a classroom for an agriculture course."
Over the next week, Tom, Mike, and John rigged up a greenhouse using some tarps and damaged tents. They made it big enough to hold

three elevated seed beds for starting plants and still have room for half a dozen students.

"Why don't you move the lettuce plants inside so we can keep them alive as long as possible since they don't store well."

Mike moved the lettuce plants inside the greenhouse along with several different squash and some radish plants.

"Mike, I understand the lettuce plants, but why the radish and squash?"

"I want to teach the kids how the different plants make their seeds so that we can have more seeds for next year."

"That makes sense. Besides, it would be a valuable teaching moment."

John left the greenhouse and headed to his own house to rest.

By the time winter showed her ugly head, the last house was completed and the garden had been harvested. Mike had done an exceptional job with the vegetables. With the help of the older boys, a small irrigation ditch was dug to automatically water the garden by simply opening a gate. The group managed to catch several wild rabbits and had them in cages where they started producing offspring. The hens were still laying eggs which produced enough to have breakfast once a week. The piglets from George were growing nicely with the female showing tel-tale signs carrying offspring. Mike was able to supply a steady supply of fresh meat which was smoked and jerked for the long winter ahead. The retention pond was well stocked with fish. There was ample supply of fruit stored away. The store house was packed. There was plenty of firewood stacked by each of the houses.

"Do you think we're ready for winter, John?"

"Ready or not, it's coming. We've spent most of our time preparing for winter. We've sorely neglected our other duties."

"What do we do now?"

"We need to prepare ourselves and our children for the coming months ahead. I think it's time to get ready for school."

The next few days, school lessons were developed according to the skills of the adults. All the basics were covered: Mathematics, English, reading, geography. Practical classes were also incorporated into the learning schedule. Woodworking, gardening, cooking, hunting and fishing. There was also seamstress and survival skills taught.

All of the children were required to attend the classes offered. Some of the older ones were allowed to teach the younger ones the basics. This freed up some of the adults to be able to give some one on one instruction for some of the more difficult subjects. This also gave the older children a sense of purpose and self esteem.

Soon, the entire community fell into a daily routine. Arise, feed the animals, eat breakfast, attend the basic classes throughout the morning and attend the practical classes in the afternoon. After school, they would eat dinner and do some chores before turning in for the night. Every seventh day, they would gather in the community house for a service where they would read from the Bible and have open discussion about its meaning.

CHAPTER 11

As the days grew shorter, the nights became increasingly colder. John noticed that the wood piles were shrinking at an alarming rate, much faster than anyone had really anticipated.

"Tom, we need to start watching the amount of wood we're burning. The stockpiles of wood are shrinking very fast. If it continues, we might have to move everyone back into the common house to conserve fuel."

"Yeah John, I noticed that too. The families all know the situation and are each responsible for their own houses."

"I realize that, but I'm more concerned with the unknown. None of us know how long the winter is going to last up here and I don't want to cause division between the families because of firewood."

"I know. Nobody knows how long we will need to stay hidden up here and I'm afraid if we don't do something proactive, we might run out of wood before this is all over."

"What do you have in mind?"

"Well John, maybe, in the spring, we could get some saplings and transplant them further up the canyon. Replant two trees for every tree we cut down."

"That's one possibility. It could give them another course of study too."

It was decided that in the spring, they would plant both hardwood and pine trees. Pine trees would be used for the immediate future and the hardwood for the distant future.

"Dad, dad, dad."

"What is it Joe?"

"Bob hurt himself really bad."

"Where is he?"

"We were exploring that cave in the back of the canyon and he cut his leg. He's bleeding really bad."

"Did you leave him up there by himself?"

"No. Billy is with him."

"Chuck," yelled John.

"Yeah John. What's up?"

"We need you. Bobby and some of the boys were playing in the cave and he cut his leg really bad. Joe thinks he might have even broken his leg."

"Let me grab my stuff and we'll go get him."

Tom, Chuck and John followed Joe back into the canyon toward the cave. When they arrived, they found Bobby sitting at the entrance crying. His pant leg was ripped from his knee to his ankle. Billy was holding a cloth on Bobby's leg trying to stop the bleeding. The snow beneath Bobby's leg was turning a bright crimson.

"What happened Billy?"

"We were exploring the cave and Bobby slipped on a rock."

"What did he cut his leg on?"

"We don't know. He just slipped and screamed. Then he started crying. Joe and I carried him out here to see his wounds. When Joe saw it, he told me to keep pressure on it and he ran to get you guys."

Chuck bent down to examine Bobby's leg while Tom and John tried to keep him from looking at his leg. There was a cut along the outside calf of Bobby's left leg. The wound was several inches long and penetrated the skin. It was deep enough to go through skin and into the muscle. Luckily, it didn't sever his calf muscle.

"What do you think?"

"Well John, Bobby here is a very lucky young man. He needs a few stitches to close his cut but he will be fine. We need to get him back to camp so we can take care of him."

They made a gurney out of a jacket and two small pine trees. Tom and John carried Bobby back to camp while Chuck walked beside Bobby keeping pressure on his leg. As they approached the camp, Chuck called out to Jill.

"Jill, can you get a needle and thread?"

"What happened?"

"Bobby cut his leg and he needs a few stitches."

When Bobby heard that, he started a whole new round of crying.

"Billy and Joe, go get me a bunch of snow. Tom, can you get some water boiling? John, I need some of that honey from storage."

First, Chuck used the boiling water to clean out the wound on Bobby's leg. Next, he used the snow to freeze Bobby's leg causing it to go numb. Next, Chuck put six stitches in to close the skin. Finally, he took some of the honey and applied it to the incision.

Why honey on the wound?"

"Honey has anti bacterial and anti fungal properties. It is a natural antiseptic. Besides, it makes the wound taste good."

"Chuck. That is a terrible thing to say. Especially to a young man like Bobby."

"Sorry Jill, just thought a little humor might make the situation more bearable."

"Bobby, everything will be fine. You just need to take it easy for a while to give that leg a chance to heal."

Once the excitement about Bobby started to subside, they noticed that Joe was covered from head to toe in some sort of black dirt.

"Joe, what do you have all over you? You look like Buckwheat from Spanky and the Gang."

Joe was covered in a fine black dust with an oily feel. There seemed to be a unique smell to it also.

"We were exploring the cave in the back of the canyon. We found an old broken wheel barrow and a lantern."

Mike came walking over from the garden, looked at Joe and said.

"Gosh Joe, you look like you came out of one of those pictures from the history books about the industrial revolution. The pictures which showed the miners from the hills of Kentucky and West Virginia. Joe, can you go back to the cave and bring back some of the black rocks? I want to experiment with them."

Joe reached into his pockets and pulled out a small handful and gave them to Mike.

"Will this be enough or do you want more?"

"That should be fine Joe, thanks."

Mike accepted the handful of rocks from Joe and walked over to the cooking fire.

"What are you thinking?"

"Well Tom, if this is what I think it is, we won't need to worry about running out of fire wood."

Mike dropped the handful of rocks onto the glowing embers of the cooking fire and waited. It took around one minute for the rocks to heat up. First, there were sparks coming from the rocks floating skyward in the smoke. Then, the rocks caught fire and started generating a lot of heat.

"Gentlemen, I think the boys found a coal mine. Let John know that we can stop worrying about running out of firewood."

Later that day, Joe led a small group of adults to the cave to determine the extent of coal and just how difficult it would be to remove. Joe led them into the back of the cave with several flashlights and they found several veins of coal running horizontally along the walls. They looked like big, black racing stripes several feet thick running on both sides of the walls.

"I think there is enough coal here to last us a few years. Maybe longer if we use it to supplement the wood supply and use it for heating just our homes."

"We can make that recommendation to the council and let them decide. We just need to be careful extracting it from here. No telling how stable this cave is if we go and start beating it with hammers and stuff."

"I'm sure we can find a way to stabilize this place in one of those books we brought."

Everyone grabbed several big pieces of coal and took them back to camp with them.

CHAPTER 12

"D AMN, THAT WAS THE last one we had."

"What happened, Jill?"

"Well Tom, we just broke the last serving spoon we had. The only thing we have left for mixing the food is sticks."

"I'm teaching the wood working class. Let me see if we can't make some new spoons for you."

"That would be wonderful."

Tom walked over to where he was teaching wood working deep in thought. Along the way, he was noticing for the first time all the things that were still needed by everyone and trying to figure out if and how they could be made from wood. There were tables and chairs, cooking utensils, bowls, and storage boxes. Tom quickly developed a course study for the children which included furniture building, fine wood working, and general repair.

Mike had also been hard at work developing his course study. Mike wanted to teach how to properly prepare the soil for planting, proper watering techniques, how and why seeds germinate, where the different seeds come from and how to properly compost.

Jill was teaching food preparation, cooking and preservation.

Martha decided to teach sewing and seamstress.

Bob was teaching how to tan the animal hides and make them into leather for everyday purposes. He also developed the course study on proper care for the animals.

All the children were required to attend the classes. They would attend their general study classes in the morning and these practical classes in the afternoon.

The adults also settled into their daily routines. There was always something that needed to be done for the community. The ruling council made recommendations as to who would teach what courses and what changes needed to be made to each course of study. It was decided that the general topics would be taught five days a week and the life studies, which the special courses were called would be taught six days. They wanted to leave one day a week for family time and play. The council also determined that they needed a spiritual leader for Sundays to lead everyone. They settled on John as their spiritual leader.

"Why me?"

"John, you're best choice we have for the position. You have the respect and admiration of everyone here. You led us here to safety and you have been a great provider for the entire community."

"I just don't think I can do it. Not with everything That I have been through."

"John, that is what makes you the perfect leader. You have the most reason to hate the outsiders but you have shown the greatest compassion and the most forgiveness of anyone here. Joe told us what happened at George's farm. He told us how you told him not to hate the bad men but to forgive them because hate is what caused this whole mess in the first place. Even when Mary was killed, you led the group to safety. You have demonstrated great personal sacrifice for the greater good. You are a living example of turning the other cheek and a great role model for the entire community."

"I just feel unworthy of such an important role. However, if it is the council's wish that I assume this position, then I will humbly accept."

"It is our desire that you assume the spiritual guidance of our homes and lives."

CHAPTER 13

"**I** WONDER WHAT TIME OF year it is?"

"That's easy. It's winter time. It's in the air every morning."

"Very funny."

"To be honest. From the amount of daylight, I would have to say that it is somewhere between Thanksgiving and Christmas."

"Thanksgiving? We totally forgot to celebrate. We need to plan a Thanksgiving meal."

"Why? What do we have to be thankful for?"

"How about for just being alive."

"Well, I guess there is that."

"Jill, can you plan a Thanksgiving meal to coincide with your cooking class and with what is in the storage?"

"I can do that. Do you think there are any turkey around? I think we have everything else in storage."

"I'll ask Mike. If not, we could use some of the chickens that are no longer laying any eggs. We should probably clear this with the council just to make sure."

The next evening, the council met for their weekly meeting.

As a general rule, the council was there to make the rules to govern the group. This meeting already had a full agenda appointing the teaching positions by who was best qualified. For the most part, everyone followed the councils directions with minimal complaints. The final appointment that the council made was to announce the John was to be the new spiritual leader. This announcement was met with a standing ovation and a long round of applause. Once the applause subsided, Bob rose to speak to the council.

"It has been discovered that we have missed the Thanksgiving holiday and would like to have the councils blessing on a little celebration."

"What do you think, John?"

"I think that as a whole, it would probably be a good idea. It would bring some semblance of normalcy here and give everyone a chance to be happy, even for just one day."

There were a few negative comments about a celebration and whether or not it was appropriate. The council listened carefully to both sides before making their decision.

"If we're going to have Thanksgiving, then we might as well as decide now about Christmas."

"How are we supposed to have Christmas? I have nothing to give my children for presents. Besides, do we really want to keep reminding our kids about what they used to have?"

It was John who spoke next.

"Well, maybe this would be a good time to remind everyone just what Christmas is really all about. For the first time, we have a chance to remove all the commercialization and focus on what Christmas is really celebrating. The birth of our Lord and Savior, Jesus Christ."

The council made the decision that both Thanksgiving and Christmas would be celebrated by the group. Not just as a reminder of where they came from but also as a promise of what is to come. After the meeting, the council spoke quietly to John.

"Do you think it is a wise decision to continue the traditions of our past lives?"

"Well, I think this will give everyone a chance to reflect not only on how their individual lives have changed since this all began but also on how their lives will continue going forward."

"Can you lead us through all this on your own or do you want our help?"

"I think I can do this on my own. I have my boys to give me inspiration and the Bible to give me guidance."

Jill started on the Thanksgiving Day meal preparations with her cooking students.

"John, Should we limit the amount of food?"

"Why?"

"We have two festivals to plan for and don't want to run out of food before spring gets here."

"Just do a small sampling of all the different foods we have. There should be something for everyone there to be thankful for. What do you have planned so far?"

"We have several different squashes, some fresh salad, chicken, rabbit, venison, and apple pie for dessert if I can get the crust to work."

"It sounds really good. You could add some fish to the menu if someone could catch them out of the pond."

Jill and her class got started on the preparations for the dinner the next day. They were careful to save the seeds from all the vegetables and give them to Mike for next spring. They were able to make a nice fresh garden salad with the help of the greenhouses. There was plenty of meat to go around and even several fish compliments of Joe.

"Jill, everything looks wonderful. Were you able to make anything for dessert?"

Well, we ran into a little problem. We didn't have enough flour to make pies so we did an apple crisp and some honey baked apple slices."

"That sounds wonderful Jill."

"John, how are your preparations going?"

"Not so well."

"What seems to be the problem? Maybe I can help."

"I just don't know if I can do this. I have so much anger and hatred inside me. How can I lead everyone in a prayer to be thankful?"

"What would Mary say?"

"She would tell me to be strong and to lead by example but I don't know if I can do that."

"John, you need to look at the big picture from our side. When we see you with all that you have endured this past year, everything you've seen, everything you've been through, and your ability to still lead us. You have been the glue that has held us together. You have taught us to trust in God and believe that something good will come out of all this. This is just a pit-stop on this journey we call life. Mary confided in me that she was dying of cancer."

"You knew?"

"Yes, I knew. She was getting progressively worse and living in increasing pain. Had she not died during our escape, she would have had a slow and very painful death that everyone here would have had to watch and be helpless to do anything about. By her dying, it allowed you to focus on the whole group. If she would have lived, you would not have been able to help all of us because you would have been focused on keeping her comfortable. Because Mary died, WE all live."

"Thank you Jill. I never would have been able to see it that way. I think I just found my inspiration."

Thanksgiving dinner was ready around four that afternoon. The entire community gathered inside the common house. For dinner, every family sat together at their own table. The council table was set up with all the food like a buffet line.

"Before we get started with this celebration, the council would like to ask our spiritual leader, John, to give us our blessing."

John slowly stood up and cleared his throat. The room became silent.

"Let us bow our heads in prayer.

> Dear Lord, We are gathered here today to give you thanks and praise. You have delivered us here to this sanctuary just like you delivered the Israelites to the promised land. You have provided us with this bounty for which we are thankful for. We give you thanks and praise for all the trials and tribulations for which only you know the reasons why and although it has been hard at times for us to endure, we put our trust in you to see us through. In all of this, we give you thanks and praise.
> AMEN."

As John sat down in his chair, the entire room remained silent and motionless.

"Dad, can we eat?"

"Sure, Joe. Lets go get some of this wonderful food."

As John rose, he looked over at Jill. There was a tear running down her left cheek. He mouthed "Thank You" to her as she smiled at him and wiped her cheek with her hand. Soon, the entire room erupted in a joyous roar. There was laughter and giggles and children singing and running around. And at least for a little while, the outside world and all its messed up problems ceased to exist.

After several hours, the celebration died down with all the families retiring to their homes. John and his boys were slowly meandering home. The sky was clear with just a sliver of a new moon showing. As they walked, a slight smile began to creep across John's face.

"Dad?"

"Yes, Patrick."

"Do you think mom would have enjoyed tonight?"

"Mom would have Loved tonight."

"I miss mommy."

"I know Joe. I miss her too. But as long as you keep her in your thoughts and in your heart, mom will be there for you."

As John was speaking, he gently touched Joe on his head and his chest. When they reached their house, they paused before entering and looked up to the sky. Just then, a meteorite went streaking across the sky in a firework fashion. Both boys gasped in amazement. John spoke silently "I Love you Mary" as a single tear rolled down his left cheek. The three of them entered the house and went to sleep.

CHAPTER 14

O NCE AGAIN, THE LITTLE community fell into its routine. The days continued to grow shorter and colder. Occasionally, there would be some snow on the ground in the mornings but it would melt away after a little while. The children continued in their studies and chores. The adults continued their work, trying to prepare for spring. They had researched in their books on how to safely extract the coal from the back of the cave. They were still getting a steady supply of meat from the healthy deer population that migrated down from the mountain tops along with an occasional cow who wandered away from George Goodwell's farm. Even though they kept sentries on the wall, they had not seen or heard anyone since Martha had joined their group earlier that fall. Tom had been training the boys in woodworking. Even some of the dads would join his class or just drop off a broken piece of furniture that needed to be repaired.

"John, what brings you here today?"

"Joe wanted a sling shot for Christmas."

"Are you going to make it for him?"

"I was hoping that maybe you had one lying around that maybe I could trade for."

"You know I don't work that way. Everyone needs to learn this skill."

"I know. I was just hoping ...."

"Maybe I could bend the rules for you just once."

"I can trade you some raw materials for it."

"John, you have done so much for us already I will make one for you to give to Joe."

"Thanks, Tom."

The council had decided that it would be easier if there was a community Christmas tree instead of everyone cutting their own so Mike transplanted a nice tree outside the community house. It was a well shaped blue spruce about seven feet tall. All the families donated item to be used as ornaments to decorate the tree. Little Susie donated her small yellow teddy bear to be used as the angel. All the teachers took time off from their normal studies to make additional ornaments for the tree and the practical application classes made presents for each other. Tom's class, being woodworking was the busiest. The older children made presents for the younger ones while learning woodworking skills. Martha's class was a close second as far as being busy for the holidays. They made a lot of dolls for the girls and leather clothing for the boys. Both classes also taught the children the art of gracious giving and receiving.

John was busy working on his Christmas message but was having trouble getting inspiration for it.

"Susan?"

"Yes, John"

"What are the little children doing for Christmas?"

"Martha, Jill and I were thinking of doing a Christmas play for everyone. What do you think?"

"I think it would be a wonderful idea. We have most of the props here already and costumes shouldn't be too hard to come up with. We could make this a Christmas tradition."

"We could. And next year, we could even have a live Christ child."

"What do you mean, Susan?"

"I'm pregnant."

"Congratulations. Have you been checked out by the doctor yet?"

"Yes, I have and he gave me a clean bill of health. He gave me a diet to follow and we set up a check up schedule."

"I am so happy for both you and Rob."

"John?"

"Yes."

"Rob and I were talking and we decided that we want to name the baby after Mary if it was OK with you?"

"I think Mary would have liked that and I would be honored and humbled if you did that."

There were many preparations that needed to be made for Christmas.

Tom taught everyone how to make bowls and cooking utensils using wood and fire. Most of the adults were making household items that they needed in their homes like tables and chairs or storage containers. The children were busy making gifts for each other. When Susan informed the council that the pageant was ready, they scheduled the Christmas celebration for the next "Sunday"

"John, are you ready for Christmas to come yet?"

"Not really."

"Everyone else is ready including Mother Nature. We have scheduled it for this coming "Sunday""

"I will be ready by then"

John had three days left to write his Christmas Prayer when he got his inspiration.

When John came out of his house Christmas morning, there was a thin blanket of snow on the ground giving everything a fresh clean look as if directly out of a Norman Rockwell painting. The sky was a deep blue without a single cloud. The smoke was rising from the chimneys of the houses and gathering high in the sky as if it were a giant balloon with eight strings anchoring it to the ground. The sun was warm on the exposed skin.

"Merry Christmas" said Joe as he emerged from his house."

"Merry Christmas son."

"It sure is a pretty morning."

"That it is."

"What are the plans for today?"

"We will have a Christmas pageant around noon followed by dinner and finally opening up presents. Why do you ask?"

"Just wondering."

Around noon, everyone gathered around the common house. There was an excitement and Joy in the air that could be felt by everyone. The Christmas tree was beautifully decorated with handmade ornaments. There was a garland made out of bright colored pieces of cloth that was tied together in rope like fashion strung all the way around the tree several times. There were lots of presents under the tree also. The children did an excellent job of making gifts for each other.

Jill and her cooking class did an excellent job of preparing a Christmas feast fit for a king. They prepared all the food and with the help of the mothers doing some of the cooking in their homes, were able to get everything ready and hot by noon.

58

While they were waiting for the signal from Susan, John decided to quiz everyone on their Christmas traditions and beliefs.

"Can anyone tell me the symbols of Christmas?"

The children started to shout out their answers.

"Tree"

"Presents"

"Star"

"Candles"

"Candy canes"

"Santa clause"

"Angels"

"Is that all?" asked John.

There was a silence from the crowd.

"what about a wreath? Or bells? Or the color Red?"

Everyone shook their heads in agreement

"Now, can anyone tell me what these symbols mean?"

There were a few mumbles from the group but no one spoke up to give an answer.

John spoke. "Let me tell you what the different symbols mean.

First, there is the tree. The Christmas tree is an evergreen. It never changes colors through the seasons which represents the unchanging hope of an eternal life through Jesus. The whole tree is always pointing heavenly to remind us that our thoughts should always be towards Jesus.

Presents represent the gifts that the three wise men gave to baby Jesus to honor him. They gave the best that they had the same way we should give our best to each other.

The Star. It was a sign of heavenly promise. God promised a Savior for the world and the star signaled the fulfillment of that promise. God always delivers on his promises. After all, it was a star that guided the wise men to where Jesus was staying.

Candles: the glow of the candle represents how we can show our thanks for Jesus. It should remind us that we need to walk in the footsteps of Jesus by doing good deeds for others.

Candy canes: These represent the shepherds who watch over their flock and guide them to safety just the way Jesus guides us in our daily lives.

Angels: The angels announced the birth of Jesus to the shepherds much the way we are called to share the good news of Jesus with others.

And finally, Santa Clause: He represents generosity. Jesus gave everything up for us. He was killed for the forgiveness of our sins that we may one day, go to heaven.

"Are there any questions?"

The group was silently pondering the words that John had just spoken. The only sounds were the gentle wind blowing through the trees and the crackling of the fire in the kitchen stove which was keeping Christmas dinner warm.

Susan came out of the common house and gave the signal that they were ready. Everyone entered the common house and found their designated table for the festivities. John was the last to enter the common house. Before going in, he carefully removed little Susie's golden teddy bear from the top of the tree.

"Come with me little buddy, you are needed inside."

As John entered there was a hush which fell upon the entire room. John just stood there in the doorway until everyone was silently looking his way.

"Let us bow our heads in prayer:

Heavenly father, We have gathered here today in celebration of your son, Jesus Christ. We celebrate the gifts he has given us and the sacrifice he made for us. We invite him to be here with us this day and everyday. To walk among us and to grant us, his grace, joy, peace and most of all, his Love. We ask that he be our beacon of hope, our guiding light, and our shining star"

With these words, John holds up the teddy bear.

"Please guide us on our path and show us the way to your kingdom in heaven and your salvation. We ask this in your name, AMEN."

The whole room responded with AMEN.

John handed the teddy bear to Susan and went to sit with his children. Next, it was Susan who got up with 10 of the children. She had chosen her "actors" by age. She used the children who were between the ages of 7 and 12 with one of the older children being the narrator. Her play was a re-telling of the Christmas story, the birth of Jesus with the teddy bear being Jesus. The play took about 20 minutes to perform and ended with the manger scene. The whole group erupted in a joyous round of applause at the end with all the actors coming center stage and taking a bow.

John stood up as the applause subsided.

"Let's give another round of applause to all the kids and the teachers who spent countless hours of rehearsals to be able to perform this Christmas pageant tonight."

The whole room broke into another round of applause. As the room quieted down again, John spoke again.

"Dear Lord, let us give thanks for this wonderful food you have provided and for the way it was beautifully prepared. May it nourish us both in spirit and body. AMEN."

With that, everyone stood up and got in line to get their food. As they came to the end of the line, they walked past the little golden bear lying in the manger to get back to their seats. Several adults and children stopped at the manger and bowed their heads in reverence to the baby in the manger.

The Christmas feast was a joyous time filled with laughter, giggles, and screams of joy. The children were chasing each other around the room playing tag. The adults were sitting around the tables engaged in small talk with each other. The older children were over in the back corner of the room playing cards and talking.

When it appeared that everyone was done eating, John stood up and announced:

"lets everyone head outside to finish up these festivities"

Everyone got up from where they were and headed outside. John was the last one to leave the common house. As he passed the manger, he bent down and picked up the teddy bear and carried it outside with him.

"Where is little Susie?"

"here I am."

"Would you be so kind as to put the star back on the top of the tree?"

"I would Love to"

John handed the little bear to Susie and then he picked her up so she could reach the top of the tree. Susie carefully placed the bear on the top of the tree and the group erupted into a loud cheer. John carefully put Susie down and she ran to her family with a giant smile on her face.

John sat in a chair next to the Christmas tree. The entire group gathered around him. All the younger children were close to him with the older children behind them and finally the parents who were warming their backs by the fire. One by one, John would reach under the tree and pull out a present and call out a name. Then, the child would need to sit on John's knee and tell everyone what they were thankful for before John would give them their present. After John called out the names of all the children, the older children presented their parents with their own gifts which consisted of needed items around the house.

CHAPTER 15

W INTER CONTINUED TO SHOW herself for a few more weeks. Everyone fell into their own routine. The men would head up to the back of the canyon once a week to mine for more coal. Rob would go beyond the wall and harvest a deer or sometimes, an elk. Mike was able to keep most of the vegetables alive inside of the greenhouses. Tom was helping everyone make furniture for their homes. Dave read how to tan the animal hides to make leather from one of the books.

John would still take excursions once in a while. He would travel mostly by steam so as to not leave a trail. Several occasions, he brought back an animal which had wandered away from George's place. Most of the time though, he was looking for animals of a different kind. John was extremely careful not to leave a trail. If there was snow on the ground, John confined his travels to the stream bed. John knew how to minimize his trail. He never left or entered the stream from the same place. He followed the stream up for several miles trying to find where Martha was attacked. He followed the stream down to where the cars were abandoned. He followed the feeder streams and tributaries for several miles both above and below the camp. He even walked along the ridge of their canyon and followed that stream for half a day. All the time, careful not to leave a trail. Always, keenly aware of his surroundings. As far as he could tell, his group was alone up here in the woods. From this vantage point, high above the canyon, John could see several highways but there was no movement. No cars, no trucks, no planes in the sky, nothing. John looked to the west to see if he could see the city. It was difficult to find at first but then, he spotted it. A wisp of smoke rising from a dark spot on the ground. So there is still some sort of life left in the town, but who was there? He said to himself. Other than the smoke to the west, John could not find any sign of life anywhere. He even looked to see if the camp was visible from this spot but could see nothing. "How many others made it out or was his, the only survivors" he wondered.

Every time, John went out, he would come back and report to the council everything he saw. One time, he discovered a wheat field that never got harvested. He snuck to the edge of the field and grabbed a pocket full of wheat kernels to give to mike. Every time, the council would listen to his report. The council would then consider the different options. After the last excursion, John recommended that several of the men plan an extended trip into town to see who was still living there. It took the council half a day to debate John's recommendation.

One of the council members came to the door.

"John, can we see you inside for a minute?"

"Sure. I'll be right there."

John entered the common house and pulled up a bench across the table from the council.

"How can I help you?"

"We feel that a trip like you are asking for would be risky right now. However, we do understand the importance of your request so we would like you to begin making preparations for a trip for up to three people to go in the late fall. However, we need for you to stay behind."

"I would really like to go on this trip."

"We know, but you have become too valuable to the entire community and we can't afford for anything to happen to you."

"I understand. I will begin to make the necessary arrangements."

John left the common house with a twinge of regret for not being allowed to go. Just then, the gate opened and Rob came through leading one of George's cows.

"Where did you find him?"

"He was down where the streams meet. I figured it would be better to slaughter him up here instead of on our front door step. Besides, it's a lot easier on me when the meat can carry itself to camp."

"This is so true. Just do me a favor and don't kill it in front of the kids. You can teach the older ones how to clean an animal and how to butcher it so as to maximize the meat but it would probably just scare the little ones."

"Will do. You look troubled. Are you OK?"

"The council wants me to plan an expedition back to town."

"Why?"

"I was on top of the mountain and could see smoke trails coming form there."

"Really?"

"Yup. They want two or three men to go this fall and investigate."

"who are you taking with you?"

"I don't get to go. They told me that I have become too important to the town's survival."

"Who are you going to pick?"

"I was thinking about asking you and Tom to go but that will have to be cleared by the council."

"maybe the council will have a change of heart by then. Truthfully, every person here is pretty valuable."

"I know."

"well, let me know if you need any help planning this. I'm always available for you if you need me."

"I do have one question for you Mike. Can you take a life if you need to?

"To protect myself or my family, absolutely."

"Let's hope that it doesn't come to that again."

With that, Rob led the cow away. John watched them walk towards the back of the camp. He looked down at the cow and then, he saw it. He yelled to Rob.

"You may not want to kill that cow Rob."

"Why?"

"She's a milker"

"I guess I should let Susan Know that we now have a source of fresh milk.

Spring was starting to show her beautiful face. The spring flowers were popping up and giving the meadow a much needed burst of color after the long and dreary winter. The snow had all melted and the stream was trying to overflow her banks. The days were getting longer and the temperature was starting to rise. The apple trees were starting to blossom and the grass was beginning to grow. The winter had not been so harsh as to be unbearable but the break of her icy grip brought a giant sigh of relief from the whole camp. The council called a general meeting for everyone so that the new duties could be distributed to everyone.

"This is what we determined needs to be done. Mike, we need you to prepare the garden for the spring crops. We can have the older children clean the animal pens and put the manure into the garden for fertilizer. Susan, please go through the pantry and find a way to preserve as much of the food as possible. As the temperature starts to rise, the food will start to spoil quickly. Tom, help everyone do the necessary repairs to their homes to make them weather proof. Those adults not specifically assigned to tasks, please help out where you can. We will still need fire wood cut and stacked. Mike will need lots of help preparing the garden for planting and there is a lot of general clean up. Are there any questions?"

"Do we have any plans for repairing clothing? My younger children are growing out of their clothes and I don't have anything to give them."

"Martha."

"Yes?"

"You are the seamstress. Do you have any suggestions?"

"We can do a clothes swap amongst the families and if we don't have the correct size, we can make them what they need. We also have the leather that has been tanned that we can make into outer gear."

"That sounds like a wonderful idea. Are there any other concerns?"

The room was quiet except for some whispering between some of the members.

"If there are no other concerns, then I think that this meeting is over."

With that, the meeting was adjouned and everyone filed out of the common house to start their spring chores. The next few weeks were filled with a flurry of activity. Mike was able to get the garden prepared and transplant some of the seedlings from the greenhouse. He then went deeper into the canyon to plant the wheat seeds that John had found. He made a small wheat field in a clearing and marked it so that the children would not run through the area and destroy the plants.

CHAPTER 16

"John."

"You seem to be in an awful big hurry Rob. What seems to be the problem?"

"Have you seen Mark? We have a big problem."

"I think he is in the back of the canyon getting coal for the fire. Why?"

"Get the council together. I need to find Mark. I'll explain everything when I get back."

Rob rushed off to find Mark. There was a fear in his eyes that John hadn't seen since they all left the city. John gathered the council together and everyone made their way into the common house to await Rob. It was cold inside so John made a fire in the fireplace and set up some chairs around one of the tables. The council was sitting at the table, going through some notes when Rob and Mark entered. There was an obvious look of dread on Rob's face. John made eye contact with Mark but Mark simply shook his head and gave a slightly fearful glance back at John.

"What is this dreadful news that you need to share with us?"

"I found someone out in the woods while I was hunting."

"What?"

"I found a man. He was injured and half dead."

John spoke next.

"Rob. Start from the beginning and tell us the whole story."

"I had shot and wounded an elk a couple of miles Southwest from here. I was following his blood trail when I crested a hill. I found a man slumped over next to a tree. I thought he was dead so I went over to him to check if he had any identification. As I was checking his pockets, he started to moan. I found his wallet and got his driver's license."

"Well? What did his license say?"

"He lives in Denver."

"What was he doing out in the woods? Where is he now?"

Rob repeated the story that the man had told him about how he lived in the suburbs of Denver. The protestors had left him alone because he looked like one of them. He was allowed to live in peace but he knew he had to get out of the area. All the basic services had stopped when the world blew up. The grocery stores ran out of food. The gas stations stopped pumping gas because they couldn't get their tanks refilled. He was able to live off the food in his freezer and the food in his garden but he knew it was time to leave when the water stopped. He was driving to San Diego to be with his family when his car broke down. So, he decided to walk. He walked for a couple of days until he got lost. He decided to follow a stream so that he would at least have water to drink. He followed the stream past a burned out farm house and that is where he fell down a hill and broke his leg. That was two days ago. He was laying there since then.

"Where is he now?"

"Right where I found him. I gave him my canteen to drink and my lunch. I told him that I couldn't move him by myself and that I would come back for him"

"Who is he?"

Rob handed over the license that he got from the man to the council. They each looked at the license carefully before handing it to the next council member.

"Thank you, gentlemen. Would you please excuse yourselves while we discuss this matter."

John, Rob and Mark all stood up and walked out of the house.

"What was the name on the license?"

"Well John, the license read Jose Ramirez."

John's face turned red and he could feel that familiar hatred rising up from the pit of his stomach. All the feelings that John had so carefully hidden in the back of his mind came rushing to the forefront. The tremendous loss of Mary. The senseless killings of so many of his friends and the utter chaos that ensued.

"John. This man had nothing to do with everything that happened."

"Mark. How can you sit here and defend this person?"

"He had nothing to do with what happened in town. I believe his story. He was too well dressed and spoke too eloquently to belong to that rabble in town."

"I don't care. I don't want him here. He can die out there in the woods for all I care."

"John, do you hear yourself? You are supposed to be our spiritual leader here. What happened to turning the other cheek or loving your fellow man? You sound like all those uneducated people in town. Kill just because of the color of their skin. I, for one, think we should bring him back here and nurse him back to health. Maybe, it would teach everyone here that they can't judge people by stereotypes but by their individual actions."

John stood there in silence, watching the flames of the cooking fire lick the logs in delicious anticipation of their inevitable meal. He allowed Mark's words sink into his mind and start to soften his soul. He knew in his mind that Mark was right but he was having a tough time convincing his heart to let go of the pain of Mary's death.

The council was having the same debate inside the common house. They were concerned about the safety of the community but trying to also believe that it was the Christian thing to do to care for the young man. After several hours of debate, they called John, Rob and Mark back into the common house.

"We have decided that we should go and get the young man and bring him back here. Rob, take Mark, Dave, and Bill with you to get him and bring him back here. John, we need you to stay here and prepare a place for him. Set up a bed for him here in the common house back there by the fire. We can use some of the animal skins to make a privacy screen for him."

Rob and his little party headed out with all the supplies they needed to stabilize Jose and carry him back safely. John worked on getting a bed ready in the common house. He got an extra cot and covered it with several blankets. He set it up close to the fireplace. He stocked up the supply of wood and set about making a privacy screen. When he had the framework completed, he went to get several animal skins from the seamstress.

"Martha, I need some of the animal skins. Do you have some extra ones I can use?"

"Sure. They are over there. What do you need them for?"

"I need to make a privacy screen in the common house."

"Why?"

"We have a guest coming. Rob found a wounded man when he was hunting today. They sent out a party to get him."

"Who is he?"

"His license says that his name is Jose Ramirez."

"And they're bringing him here?"

"The council decided."

"Are they crazy? Do they realize just who is hunting us?"

"I'm not happy about this any more than you are, but the council decided and we must follow their rules"

"But John? How am I supposed to welcome this person after what me and my family have been through? And what about you? Can you honestly stand there and tell me that you want this person here after everything you have been through?"

"I know, Martha. Part of me would have left him out there in the woods to die a slow and painful death. A little poetic justice for all the pain and suffering we have gone through. But part of me believes that he was brought to us by a higher power to help us onto the path of healing. Through him, we can learn to forgive all the evil that has happened in our lives. The evil that brought all of us to this canyon. As the spiritual leader here, I want to believe that this is for the greater good for everyone involved."

"Maybe you're right. Maybe he was brought to us so that we can learn to forgive. The skins are over in the corner. Take whatever you need."

"Thanks, Martha."

John grabbed several skins from the pile and headed back to the common house. There was an excitement in the air about Rob and his discovery. John could hear several small groups of people talking but he couldn't quite make out the words. He knew he was the topic of their conversations because as he approached, they all stopped and watched him go by. Everyone was trying to read his facial expressions without actually talking to him. Once across the compound, John headed inside the common house to finish making the emergency quarters for their guest. All the while, he was praying that God would give him the words to speak. Words that could convey forgiveness and acceptance of Jose. As John was finishing, Joe came into the room.

"Dad, did you hear?"

"Yeah Joe, I heard."

"What was the council thinking by bringing him back here? Don't they know what this person represents?"

"The council knows exactly what this person represents. They also know that it is our Christian duty to bring him back here and nurse him back to health. Don't you remember the story of the good Samaritan?"

"But dad."

"No buts about it. The council discussed it for several hours and weighed all the options. It was their decision to help him and we must obey. If we start to put our personal feelings and desires above the good of the community, then we will all fail here. Besides, if there are more out there, he might be able to tell us."

"How are you dealing with this?"

"With a lot of prayer and reflection. Joe, I want you to approach this with an open mind. Try and not let the past cloud your perceptions of who this person is. Look past his skin color."

"That's easier said than done."

"I know son, but try and do it anyway."

The words flowed easily from Johns lips and even though they were filled with truth, he was not sure if he truly believed them. Joe left the common house with his dads words filling his ears and weighing heavy on his heart. Joe turned at the door and looked back at his father.

"Dad, I'll try and do as you want but it won't be easy."

"I know son, nothing worth while ever is easy."

Joe turned back around and left. John went back to work to finish all of his preparations. It was another hour before Rob and his party returned with Jose. They had made a litter out of a sleeping bag and two small trees. Dave had made a splint out of some sticks and rope. They stabilized the leg and cleaned the wound as best they could before transporting back to camp. Once inside the walls, they brought him over by the kitchen area and set his litter on the ground. Between the pain of manipulating the bones back into place, being dehydrated, and the bumpy ride back to camp, Jose laid there motionless on the ground. Dave and Susan went to work cleaning him up with soap and hot water. Mark was busy going through his pockets and his belongings looking for any sort of identification. They removed his clothing down to his boxers and carefully checked him out. They cleaned and bandaged all his scrapes and cuts. Dave carefully checked his splinted leg to make sure that the break didn't slip out of position during transport. Finally, they covered him with several blankets and skins. They moved him into the common house and carefully placed him into the bed that John had made. They started a small fire in the fireplace and placed a glass of water on the table by the bed. Bill brought over a chair and sat down next to him.

CHAPTER 17

"I'LL TAKE THE FIRST watch."

"Thanks, Bill. Give him two of these pills when he wakes up and have him drink all the water."

"What are these?"

"Tylenol. It will help with the pain and swelling."

"Thanks Doc. I'll make sure he takes them."

"Come get us when he wakes up."

"Will do Doc."

Everyone left the common house except Bill. They all gathered around Mark who was sitting by the fire place, going through all of Jose's belongings.

"Mark, What did you find out by going through his stuff?"

"There is a wedding picture of him so he has a wife someplace. He lives in Aurora Colorado. He has keys to a Toyota and a Beemer. There is a letter from a Mr. Banks addressed to a Mr. and Mrs. Ramirez with a return address in Lemon Grove, Ca. He has an ID card for the Budweiser plant. There are several credit cards and a voter ID card. Everything has his name on it. His duffel bag has clothes and a shaving kit inside."

"Was there anything else?"

"No. Everything seems to confirm what he told Rob. I think he was just in the wrong place at the wrong time and he suffered some really bad luck."

"Should we put a guard on him?"

"I don't think he is going to go anywhere, at least not with that leg. We should probably have someone sit with him in case he needs something during the night. At least, until he starts feeling better."

"Mark, do we need another bed set up or will the chair be sufficient for now."

"I think the chair should be good for now."

Dave went back into the common house to check on his patient and to tell Bill what was discussed. When he came out, he informed the council that Jose was awake long enough to take the medicine and drink the water but he fell back asleep. The council decided to talk with him the following day.

Life went back to normal for the community. Jose slept for three days waking up just long enough to drink some water and take some Tylenol. The men all took turns watching over Jose at night while the women would watch him during the day. The council moved its meeting place to around the kitchen fireplace where they could discuss any of the issues that came up. Mike finished getting the garden planted and with the irrigation ditch that was dug the previous year, he could water the entire thing in a matter of a couple of hours. Rob was still very successful at gathering meat and would take some of the older children to teach them the finer points of hunting. Susan was able to find ways to keep the food from spoiling. She started by having all the available snow gathered up and placed inside the pantry. She dried some of the fruit and vegetables. The meat was smoked or turned into jerky. The children were busy taking care of the animals. They would pick grass and flowers from the field for feed for the rabbits, and cow. The pigs were fed the leftover food scraps. When Jose finally gained enough strength back, the council went in to have their talk with him.

The council came into the common house carrying a plate of food. Mike had just finished changing the bandages on Jose's wounds.

"We brought you some breakfast. Can you eat?"

"I can try. Where am I"?

"You are safe with us and that is all you need to know right now".

"How did I get here"?

"We found you in the woods".

"But how......"

It was Rob who cut him off. "Why don't you let us ask you the questions and you just lay there and answer them".

Jose laid back with a small nod of his head.

"What were you doing in the woods"?

"I was trying to reach my in-laws in California. I promised my wife before she died that I would go and keep them safe".

"How did you wind up in the woods"?

"I was taking the backroads from Denver to L.A. to try and avoid the rioters when I had car trouble. So I started walking. I found a small stream and started following it. I figured that everything needed water to drink, including me so if I stuck to the stream, I might find some food. I didn't find much in the ways of animals but the spring plants were starting to bloom which gave me roots and plants to chew on. I was following it for several days, walking along a game path of sorts. By this time, I was a little weak from lack of food. There was a sudden noise behind me which startled me. When I turned around, my foot got caught on something and I tripped and fell down an embankment. My leg must have hit something really hard on the way down because there was a sharp pain. I don't really remember much after that. I think I tried to crawl to the stream but it is nothing but a hazy dream. That is the last that I remember until woke up here. I'm not sure that I appreciate this line of questioning".

"Let me tell you this. We don't really care WHAT you appreciate or don't appreciate. With everything that has gone on with the world lately, you should just be thankful that we didn't leave you out there to die in the woods. We have to protect our families the best way that we know how so if this line of questioning is bothering YOU, we can always put you back where we found you."

"I guess that I should be thankful that you have taken care of me this far".

"After everything we have seen, we debated for a long time on whether or not to just leave you in the woods".

"You can't hold ME accountable for what happened to you? My family has lived in Texas since before it became part of the U.S. My family has fought and died for this country in every war since the war of 1812. My own wife was killed because she was white and in the wrong place at the wrong time. I promised her that if anything ever happened to her, I would find her parents and help them any way I could. I can't even speak the language."

"Please understand. We are doing what we feel is best for the whole community. We need to protect the compound and everything that is contained here. Our entire lives here depend on the security of this place. You can't fault us for wanting to stay safe?"

"So, why did you bring me here if you were worried about the safety of everybody?"

"It was the Christian thing to do. You see, We feel that you were brought to us as a way to start the healing process. If we can learn to accept you for who you are and not just a person of different skin color. Then, maybe we can learn to look past the pain and hatred and accept that everyone should be judged by who they are and not how they look."

"I guess that I should be thankful for you rescuing me and nursing me back to health. I just don't know how I can help you regain your trust in humanity. I am just one man with a broken leg."

"Let us worry about how to make this work. You just get better."

With that, Jose started eating his breakfast. The council left the lodge in single file through the door. John was last in line to leave. He paused at the door, looked over his shoulder back at Jose, shook his head slowly and left. Jose was alone with Susan.

"That man really hates me. Doesn't he?"

"John lost his wife during our escape up here. She was shot by one of THOSE people while trying to run the blockade. She is buried down on the mountain side."

"Maybe, he should talk to your priest about how to learn to forgive. He needs it badly."

"He IS our spiritual advisor."

Jose laid back down on his bed. The feeling of dread slowly overcoming his body.

CHAPTER 18

L IFE SLOWLY WENT BACK to normal. The adults took turns caring for
Jose in addition to doing their own daily duties. Jose was slowly gaining
his strength back. When it was John's turn, he brought Jose some breakfast,
set it on the table and turned to leave.

"John?"

John slowly turned around to face Jose.

"What?"

"John, I see that you are hurting. I can see it in your eyes."

"So"

"John, I'm hurting too. I also lost someone dear to me in this mess."

A look of doubt slowly creeped across John's face.

"My wife was killed by a gang who was robbing the store that she was
in. She had asked me to go and get some flour because she was making a pie
for me for my birthday. I told her that I would do it later because I was busy
watching TV. She told me to never mind, that she would go do it herself.
She left before I could even tell her that I Loved her. When she didn't come
home, I drove to the store thinking that I would find her in the parking lot
with car trouble. As I drove down the street, I saw all the flashing lights
in front of the store. I pulled into the parking lot only to have a policeman
frantically waving at me. I parked my car in one of the few open spots along
the fence. As I got out of the car, a policeman told me that I couldn't go in.
I asked him what had happened and he explained that there was a robbery
at the store and they had killed all the customers inside before they left.
When I explained that my wife was inside, he grabbed me with both hands

and wouldn't let me go. After what seemed like an hour, he looked me in the eyes and explained that there were NO survivors. I had to follow the ambulances to the hospital so that I could I.D. her body."

"I am sorry for your loss. I didn't know. I too have lost someone very special to me."

"I know. Susan told me that you lost your wife trying to escape."

"Then, you know why I feel such hatred towards you."

"I didn't have anything to do with your wife dying other than the color of my skin."

"I know, but it doesn't make it any easier with you being here. You are the personification of everything bad that has happened to us. We have come to hate you simply because of how you look. We even contemplated leaving you out in the woods to die."

"Well, I am certainly glad that you didn't do that."

"Hopefully, together, we can start a healing process. I am trying to raise my boys to overcome hate while at the same time, lead this group spiritually to look for goodness in the situation."

"At least you have the reassurance that your wife will be waiting in Heaven for you when you get there."

John looked at Jose with a puzzled expression on his face. "Why do you say that?"

"Because, the greatest act of Love is to sacrifice yourself for someone else. Your wife gave her life saving the lives of others. She got an all-expense paid trip straight to Heaven. Did you get to say good bye to her?"

"Yes. I did get so say good bye and that I Loved her."

"That's more than I got."

As John looked at Jose, his expression slowly changed from disgust to sorrow. He turned and walked towards the door. When he reached it, he stopped, turned back around. "Eat your food. You're going to need your strength. You have a lot of chores that need to be done. After all, you can't stay in our common house forever."

With that, John turned back around and left. Jose ate his food in silence, a feeling of relief slowly covering his body.

A few days later, the council was sitting by the kitchen fireplace discussing the problems that seem to keep arising. They were trying to figure out why the wheat seeds were not germinating properly.

"There is not enough nutrients in the soil where we planted the wheat. We need to add some fertilizer to it".

"But Mike, what do we add to it? It's not like we can go to Home Depot and buy wheat fertilizer".

"Add the chicken shit to the soil".

Everyone turned around to see Jose standing near the doorway. He was using the crutches that Tom had made for him.

Mike spoke "what did you say Jose"?

"I said, add the chicken shit to the soil. The ground around here is not acidic enough to support good growth for the wheat".

"How do you know that"?

"I worked for Budweiser. I was in the lab where we tried to get better yields from our hops and barley. We discovered that the more acidic the soil, the better yields we got from the crops. By adding the chicken shit and some pig shit to the soil, it will become more acidic and thereby yield better crops with a higher percentage of seed germination. You will just have to be careful that you don't add too much or the ground will become too acidic and actually burn up the sprouts".

"Well, we can't add too much. We don't have that many chickens".

"So, you have a green thumb"?

"Maybe a little bit of one".

"Would you mind helping Mike with the garden? He could use some assistance keeping everything growing".

"If Mike would like my help, I would be happy to help him out. I need to get out and start building my strength anyway. John told me that I have a lot of chores to do once I get my strength back".

CHAPTER 19

T HE MEETING BROKE UP and mike led Jose to the green house where he could get a good look around. The pace there was slow going due to Jose trying to traverse the uneven, muddy ground with his crutches. Several times, the tips got stuck as they sunk into the mud under his weight. They had to go the long way around because the bridge across the dam was too narrow to navigate with crutches.

"This is a nice encampment you have here".

"Yeah, we were lucky to find it. John found it when he was hunting several years back. He followed a wounded deer and it lead him straight to this clearing. Who knew that a deer would be our savior."

"Were all these little huts here or did you have to build them yourselves"?

"We built them once we got here. Each family had to build their own big enough for their entire family. Once you get stronger, you'll need to build one too. Don't worry though, everyone pitches in to help. We all have our special gift that we share with the community".

As they arrived at the green house, Mike pulled back the flap to the tent. "And this is my special gift". Inside, there were all the seedlings of this years garden growing in raised beds. Jose stepped inside and allowed his eyes to adjust to the shadows.

"I'm impressed. There looks to be enough plants to feed a small army".

"Army? No. But a small community, hopefully. And with enough left over plants to produce seeds for next year."

"How are you preparing the soil"?

"We use the animal droppings that we gather when we clean their pens. We work it into the soil when we plant the seedlings and we will do it again in the fall after we harvest all the plants"

"That sounds like a lot of work but it is the right approach to keep the soil with the proper nutrients".

"How do you keep the food from spoiling"?

"Once we pick it, we store it inside a cave by the kitchen. It seems to keep pretty well, all things considered. Any of the food that does go bad gets fed to the pigs along with the table scraps from cooking".

"Have you tried honey"?

"we use honey as a sweetener. We also use it as an antiseptic when someone gets hurt".

"Really"?

"We used it on you when you showed up. You had lots of scrapes and cuts all over your body. We just spread it on your cuts and bandaged you up. Your cuts healed in about a week with very little infection".

"Well, I mean have you tried to use honey as a preservative"?

"As a preservative"?

"Yes. The Egyptians used to use it to preserve their food. It has some type of antifungal properties that make it a great preservative".

"No kidding? I'll let the council know about that. It sure would cut down on the amount of food that goes bad. Better yet. Why don't YOU tell the council about it. Might help convince them that it was the right thing to do to bring you inside with us."

"Do you think it will help John change his mind about me"?

"John has had a lot of bad stuff happen to him and he is still trying to deal with it"

"I know. Several people have already filled me in. Do you think that he will ever come to terms with what happened?"

"Will you ever come to terms with your tragedy? It seems to me that you and John share a common bond. Maybe that will be enough to bring him around."

"only time will tell."

Mike and Jose stood there in the opening of the seedling tent in silence for several minutes. The deeper meaning of their verbal exchange slowly taking root in their souls. Mike was the first to break the silence.

"So, how did the Egyptians use honey to preserve their food?"

"It was a simple process really"

Jose showed Mike how to prepare the honey solution similar to what the Egyptians did.

"After the solution is ready, you just coat the fruits and vegetable with this and then store it in a cool, dry place like a cave."

The next day, Jose went through the whole process with the council.

"Do you think this will work?"

"The Egyptians were doing it for hundreds of years before refrigeration was ever invented. Besides, it has to be better than what you are doing now to preserve your food which is nothing"

"We can try it. Would you mind showing Susan how to do it?"

"I would like that. What else do you do to store your food for the winters?"

"We store it inside a cave to help keep it cool."

"How are you keeping the cave cool?"

"We gather up the snow and put it on top of the food inside the cave. It helps to prolong the life of the food."

"What about ice?"

"What do you mean?"

"A long time before there were refrigerators, there were ice boxes. These were storage boxes and they put a block of ice in the top of the box and that would keep everything inside cool. You could use the cave as a giant ice box by putting blocks of ice in one corner of the cave and it would keep the whole cave cool. Does your pond ever freeze over?"

"Not all the way due to the current but the edges of it freeze pretty thick."

"If you cut the ice from the edges of the pond and put it inside the cave, it will preserve the food better."

When the meeting ended, Jose went over to show Susan how to prepare the fruit and vegetables for dipping into the preservative. He then checked out the storage cave to see what recommendations he could give them there.

"If you build a low wall in front of the opening, you could trap the cold air inside of the cave which would help keep it cooler in here."

There wasn't much left over from last years harvest to preserve but they did the best that they could.

Mike had finished preparing the fields for planting and added the chicken droppings to the wheat field just as Jose had recommended.

Jose was getting stronger by the day and the more he was around, the more the people began to like him. John kept his distance but as he continued to observe the little community, he noticed the gradual change in the attitudes of the others. Even his own sons were treating Jose with respect and kindness.

Jose noticed the change in the people almost immediately. They were no longer looking down their noses with suspicion at him but were starting to engage him in small talk. They were eager to know his life story and all the bigotry he had experienced growing up. He told them about how his first house was vandalized when he first got married. How the police only did a hap-hazard investigation into the incident because they knew the culprits were a group of high schoolers. Then he told them he felt betrayed by the justice system when the kids only received community service for spray painting Nazi Swastika's all over the exterior of the house just because one of the kids was the son of the local sheriff. The bigotry and hatred he felt was so bad that he decided to move from his small town into the suburbs of Denver. Jose then told them how he was welcomed into his new neighborhood where he got a job with the Budweiser corporation and what a difference a large city was compared to a small town. Jose really liked the diversity that the large city offered and how he felt accepted there being in a mixed marriage with a white wife. All of his neighbors were friendly. They would all bar-b-que on the weekends and play basketball in the streets. All the kids in the neighborhood went to the same school and they all hung out together. Everyone would help each other whenever any issue came up. Then, one day, it all changed.

"John?"

"Yes Jose?"

"Can we talk?"

"Sure. What's on your mind?"

"I know that you had nothing to do with my wife being killed but I have a real issue finding forgiveness in my heart for what happened."

"Well, we had nothing to do with the death of your wife so don't try to blame us."

"Exactly my point John."

John stood there in silence, suddenly realizing how wrong he had been in affixing the blame for Mary's death on Jose simply based on his skin color. A tear began to roll down John's cheek as he turned and faced Jose.

"Jose, you are so right and I am so sorry for blaming you for the death of my wife. Can you ever forgive me?"

"I forgive you John and maybe together, we can lead the rest of these people to find forgiveness and healing."

"I would like that."

The next Sunday, John announced in his sermon that they would be doing a series on forgiveness.

"Let us turn to Matthew 6:14-15 and read from the scriptures."

Everyone opened their bibles to the gospels and read silently. When they were finished reading, all their eyes were focused on John.

"You all know the trials and tribulations that have brought us to this place. Everyone here has suffered greatly and endured the wrongs brought upon us by society. Our hearts have been filled with hatred for a people we don't even know. I myself, your elected spiritual leader has had my own heart hardened with the death of Mary. Our Loving God saw this happening to us so he sent us a way out. He Sent to us, Jose. Jose did not come to us as a sacrificial lamb for us to extract our revenge. NO, I say. Jose came to us as a helpless creature of God. Someone who needed us to care for him. Someone who needed our nurturing in order to survive much the same way as a baby needs the nurturing of its mother. It is my belief that God has sent Jose to us so that we could learn to Love again. But so long as hatred is in our hearts, Love cannot grow. So, today, we pray that God takes this hatred from us and the first steps of this journey is to ask for forgiveness. So, Jose, would you please stand up?"

Jose stood up from his chair in the front row. Jose and John faced each other.

"Jose, I ask you this question in front of my God and in front of my peers: Can you find it in your heart to forgive me?"

"I forgive you and ask that you forgive me also."

"I forgive you."

With that, Jose and John embraced each other.

Over the next few weeks, John and Jose spent a lot of time together. John would help Jose and Mike with the gardens and then, they would go off alone someplace quiet to talk. It was rumored that they didn't want the rest of the group to see them cry as they worked through their grieving process. John would read different scriptures and then they would discuss them. After a while, John would invite his children to join them in their discussions to help them to grieve. Soon, the whole group began to notice the change in John. He was smiling more often and he seemed to find some real Joy in his situation.

"Jose, you need to start building your own house soon. You can't live in our common house forever."

"Truthfully John, I was thinking that I really need to continue on my journey. I made a promise to my wife to look after her parents if anything ever happened to her. I still need to fulfil that promise."

"You realize that they are most likely dead?"

"I know but I need to try. I have to know for certain, for my wife's sake."

"Fair enough, what can we do to help you?"

"All I need are some provisions and a general direction to get down from this mountain."

"Let me talk to the council and see what kind of arrangements can be made."

The next day, John spoke with the council to inform them of Jose's plans. They decided to assist Jose with food, water, and a map and compass. It took several days to gather up all the provisions for Jose. The group was saddened to see him go but they understood his reasoning.

"Are you sure that you don't want to stay? We would love it if you became a member of our community."

"No. I really need to finish my quest."

"I can guide you to a road nearby if you want?"

"That would be a great help."

John and Jose walked out through the gate and headed towards George's house. The rest of the group all shook Jose's hand as he left and wished him a safe journey.

Later in the day, John returned to camp.

Over the next few weeks, life once again returned to normal. The busyness of the spring planting was finally over only to be replaced with the monotonous routine of summer repairs. There was wood to be gathered and cut, coal to be mined, honey to be collected, homes to be fixed. The list went on and on.

CHAPTER 20

"D O YOU HEAR THAT?"

"Yeah, it's been going on for two days. I think they found the cars."

"I think so too. I just wonder who they are."

"There's only one way to find out. I'll go have a look and find out who "they" are.

Do you want some company?"

"No, I'll just tell them I'm going to go see Mary. That way, it won't raise any suspicion. While I'm gone, quietly start getting things ready just in case we need to move in a hurry."

John headed out through the gate and followed the stream as he had done so many times before. Everyone was used to him leaving for several days at a time. Sometimes, he would take his boys down to see mom but most of the time, he went solo. Everyone knew John was still grieving the loss of Mary so they just let him go so that he could work through his grief in private.

John headed down the stream as he had done so many times before. Stepping gingerly on the rocks as he went, he was able to make quick time by staying in the water. As John got closer to the old bridge, the sounds of helicopter became more frequent until it was almost a constant thump, thump, thump from above. Whoever "they" were, they were not trying to be quiet. John approached the area by the old bridge with caution. He could see a military style camp set up close to the road at the entrance of the two-track. There were fifteen tents with a dozen vehicles all parked in a line. There were several trailers placed in a circle with men coming in and out of on a regular interval. There were several sentries posted in different locations all walking their posts as if they were dreaming. John needed to find a way inside the camp to discover who they were and what they wanted. John located one sentry off by himself and he decided to make him his ticket inside the camp.

John made his way around to the lone sentry. He picked up several stones which he could use as a diversion. John waited for the sentry to pass him and he threw the stones over the sentry and into the brush on the other side. The sentry stopped and faced the noise. John moved in toward the sentry. With his left hand, John covered the sentry's mouth so he couldn't scream. With his right hand, John covered the sentry's side arm so that he couldn't pull his weapon. With his left leg, John knocked out the sentry's knees so that he fell, face first into the sandy ground. John landed on top of the sentry, covering the young man's body with his own. John quickly looked around to see if anyone had seen the poor sentry go down. There was a look of sheer terror in the young man's eyes as John spoke.

"Are you American?"

The young man shook his head in affirmation.

"Are you hurt?"

The young man shook his head no.

"I'm going to remove my hand from your mouth, don't scream."

The young man shook his head no.

John slowly removed his hand.

"What's your name?"

"Private first class Jones."

"Well private first class Jones, what are you doing out here?"

"Looking for survivors."

"Survivors? From what?"

"Survivors from the great cleansing."

"Who's in charge?"

"Captain Baker is in charge."

"Where's his tent?"

"Over there."

The private shrugged his head in the direction of one of the tents near the edge of the encampment.

John removed the pistol from the private's holster and then helped him up off the ground.

"If you're telling me the truth, nobody will get hurt but I'll keep this until I know for sure. Let's go."

John and private Jones made their way back into the woods. They walked around the camp quietly until they were directly behind the command tent. They could hear voices coming from everywhere. They listened until the voices left the command tent, then they crept to the back of the tent where John took his knife and sliced open the back of the tent.

"Come on private Jones," John whispered, "get inside here and be quick about it."

The private stepped through the opening first followed by John. Inside the tent, there were two desks at ninety degrees to each other. The far side of the tent was lined with six chairs. There was a light hanging from the center support post. Each desk had a chair behind it and a small lamp sitting on top of it. The desks were cluttered with maps of the area.

"Private, kneel down next to that post, cross your ankles, put your hands on top of your head and lace your fingers together."

Private Jones did as he was commanded. John started looking through the maps on the desks. One map was of particular interest. It showed an area circled where the old bridge was. Next to the circle, there was a cross drawn in pen.

"Damn, they found Mary." John whispered to himself. "private Jones" John whispered, "we're going to wait until your Captain Baker returns. Don't do anything stupid and nobody will get hurt. Right now, I need some answers."

John sat down behind the desk closest to the tent wall. He turned out the light so as to make himself less visible. The two of them waited there in silence for what seemed like an eternity but in reality was just twenty minutes. Finally, there were two voices coming toward the tent. John couldn't make out the words but he knew the tone of voice. It was the voice of command. The front tent flap flew open and two men stepped inside. As the flap closed behind them, Captain Baker began to speak.

"What the hell?"

John quickly silenced them with "ssh"

"Gentlemen, please be quiet and sit over there."

The two officers looked in the direction of the voice and stared down the business end of private Jones's pistol. They slowly moved in the direction of the chairs and sat down keeping several chairs between them.

"Very good, gentlemen."

"Who do we have the pleasure of sitting behind my desk?"

"I'll ask the questions first if you don't mind. What are you doing up here in the woods?"

"We're looking for survivors of the cleansing war. We were told that there was a group up here in the mountains."

"Who told you that we were here?"

"We were told about you by a man called Jose Ramirez. He said that he was helped by a group up here when he broke his leg. He gave us a general location but was a little fuzzy on the specific location."

"So, it's over? Who won? How did it end?"

"Yes, it's over. Al-Queda lost. It took almost two years, but Al-Queda was hunted down and eliminated by the rest of the world. As far as winners, there's never a winner in war, only survivors and losers."

"I noticed that you have an area next to the old bridge circled."

"Yes, we found some evidence of survivors."

"What did you find?"

"We found several vehicles belonging to a group who managed to get out without getting killed."

"What's this X here for?"

John indicated the cross marked on the map.

"That Sir, is a grave marker."

Suddenly, John could feel his face becoming red with anger.

"You didn't desecrate that grave, did you?"

"No sir, you have my word of honor on that. The grave was not disturbed in any way. I would have personally shot any of my men who would have done such a heinous act. Now, we have answered your questions. It's time you answered a few. To start with, who are you?"

"My name is John."

"John Smith?"

"How would know that?"

"We were able to run the registration on the vehicles we found. One of the cars belonged to a John and Mary Smith. From the looks of the cars, you people were lucky to get out with your lives."

"Most of us were lucky. Do you have a chaplain with you?"

"Yes, we do."

"Private Jones" said John, "would you be so kind as to get the chaplain?"

"Just the chaplain" commanded Captain Baker.

"Yes sir" spoke private Jones.

Private Jones got up from the ground, rubbed his knees a little and excused himself out through the tent flap.

"That's a good man there," said John.

"How many escaped with you into the woods?"

"There were a total of thirty five who left down there. Thirty four made it to safety."

"Who is buried by the cars?"

"My wife, Mary."

"How many of you are there now?"

"There is a total of thirty eight of us."

Suddenly, there was a knock at the front of the tent.

"Captain Baker? You wanted to see me?"

"Yes chaplain, please come in."

the chaplain stepped through the tent flap followed by private Jones.

"Chaplain, this is John Smith. He has been gracious enough to bring our mission to an early and successful ending."

John stood up to shake hands with the chaplain. He suddenly realized that he still had the pistol pointed at the officers.

"Oh, sorry about that. Here, private Jones, I believe this belongs to you."

John handed the pistol back to the private butt first. He then shook hands with him and then with the chaplain.

"It's a pleasure to meet you Mr. Smith. Where are the rest of your group?"

"They are in a canyon about two days walk from here. Captain, if you put together a small scouting party, we can go get them in the morning."

"What kind of assistance do you think you need to get everyone down from there?"

"I think just some medical personnel to give everyone a quick check up, some guards to help with some of the elderly coming back, and the chaplain to perform some of his works."

"Any one else?"

"Just yourself captain. That is unless you just want to wait here until we get back?"

"Not on your life."

"XO, you will stay here with the majority of the company until we get back."

"Can you be ready to go by morning?"

"We'll be ready."

"Chaplain, would you please accompany me to say a blessing for my wife?"

"I would be honored."

John and the chaplain left to go visit Mary. As they left, John could hear the XO and Captain Baker making plans for tomorrow. John walked next to the chaplain in silence, guiding him the short distance to Mary. Once there, the chaplain made a sign of the cross and said a short prayer asking God to receive the spirit of Mary Smith into his arms and blessing her. Afterward, the chaplain assured John that Mary was in Heaven watching over them.

"How do you know that she made it?"

"Anyone who gives their life so that others can live, get an express ride straight through the pearly gates."

The words were reassuring to John.

CHAPTER 21

T HE NEXT MORNING, JOHN led the small group of soldiers into the woods and for the first time, John didn't worry about whether or not he left a trail that someone could follow. They walked for two days following the stream until they came to a feeder stream that led to a box canyon. They followed that feeder stream for about a quarter mile. They went around a bend in the small stream and stopped just short of the wooden fence. John had everyone stay back so as not to get accidentally shot by one of the guards. The guards were expecting John to be alone.

"Hello in the camp, it was John speaking loud enough for the sentries to hear."

"Hey John, you sure did make enough noise. You sounded like there were six or seven of you."

"Well, actually I found a little surprise for everyone. Open the gate and for God's sake, don't shoot."

"Don't shoot who?"

"I brought some guests home for dinner."

The sentries opened the gate and six soldiers stepped out of the woods, into the stream, and through the gate.

"Tom, gather up everyone, they're going to want to hear this."

Tom gathered everyone in the compound around the kitchen area. John went into the common house and brought out a chair for the captain.

"Everyone, this is Captain Baker and his men. They have been looking for us for several weeks and they bring great news."

There was a gasp from everyone in the crowd. All of the sudden, there were questions bombarding the guests from every direction. Tom held up his hands to try to quiet the group.

"All of your questions will be answered if you just give him a chance to speak."

Captain Baker decided to stand on the chair so that his voice would carry over the crowd. This also gave him a more domineering presents among them.

"First, let me tell you that the crisis is over and you have nothing more to fear. My men and I are here to escort you all back to the safety and security of the new society."

"How did it start?"

"As you all are aware, Al-Queda launched a plan to eliminate every Caucasian on the planet and they wanted to start with America first. You all witnessed it first-hand that fateful morning so long ago. America was invaded from both her borders and every white person was targeted for elimination."

"How long did it last?"

"Initially, the world leaders condemned the actions but did little to stop any of the bloodshed. It took over a year for anyone to come to the aid of us. However, once the world economies started to collapse, the world as a whole hunted down Al-Queda and eliminated them completely from the planet. Every country sent troops to our aid and helped to remove the insurgents by diplomatic measures first and later by force."

"How far did they get before they got stopped?"

"By far, the greatest damage was done in the southwest. They got as far north as San Francisco with the line going through Las Vegas, Albuquerque, Amarillo, Oklahoma City, Dallas, Houston. The ones that came from Canada? Well, just say they didn't know most the people up north carried guns with them. And, because they struck America first, when it started in other countries, those countries were ready for it and stopped it quickly."

"How many people died?"

"There were a total of four and a half million people killed during this terrible act. Three and a half million Caucasians, and one million aggressors. There were also half a million taken as prisoners who will stand trial for their crimes."

"Who is going to punish those people?"

"The aggressors have been taken to prisons around the world and they will be tried in whatever country they are in. and, they will be tried by those countries laws. The United Nations decided that it would be the best solution. That way, the burden doesn't fall to just one place. It is my guess that most of them will be put to death for their crimes in whichever country they were sent to."

"Does this mean we can go home?"

"I have been instructed to find any survivors and bring them back to civilization. Where you go from there is entirely up to you. But don't be surprised if home has changed. It is my understanding that your town was burned to the ground by those people. I know you all have been here a long time but I would like to head back come first light. This has been a long deployment for me and I miss my family."

"I guess it's settled, we leave in the morning."

"What does the council say about this?"

"We decided that this should be an individual decision. This danger has been eliminated so there is no longer a need for us to make your decisions for you. Everyone is free to choose."

Everyone talked amongst themselves and decided to return to the city and start over. John was the only one who decided to stay.

"John, are you sure you want to stay? We don't have to live like this anymore."

"I'm sure Tom. My boys and I are going to stay. The good Lord has provided a good life for us out of this location. There is nothing left down there for us. Besides, Mary is up here. We have everything we need. Fresh water, food, shelter, and peace and quiet."

Printed in the United States
By Bookmasters